Magic for Beginners

A Charity Anthology for Kids

**Edited by Amber M. Simpson
& Madeline L. Stout**

Cover © 2019, GermanCreative

"Damara and the Pirates" © 2019, Rebecca Buchanan
"The Magic Fork" © 2019, Liam Martin
"Mollie's Magic Book" © 2019, Margaret Bailes
"The Magic Within" © 2019, Zoey Xolton
"Birthday Magic" © 2019, Sofi Laporte
"Toadstone" © 2019, Vonnie Winslow Crist
"The Feathered Cloak" © 2019, Edward Ahern
"The Marvelous Sweet Shop With No Name" © 2019, Rima El-Boustani
"The Beginning of a Legend" © 2019, Bella Guerra
"Cookies and Milk" © 2019, Eddie D. Moore
"No Fireballs at the Kids' Table" © 2019, Rennie St. James
"Miss Phillips" © 2019, Christine King
"Queen Zoe and the Spinning Game" © 2019, Randee Dawn
"Unicorn Saturday" © 2019, Carol Ann Martin
"Cindy Lee the Incredible" © 2019, Dan Fields
"Finally, Magic" © 2019, Sofi Laporte
"The Lolly Bag" © 2019, Amani Gunawardana
"Finders Keepers" © 2019, Kelly A. Harmon

Editor-in-Chief: Madeline L. Stout

Fantasia Divinity Magazine & Publishing
www.fantasiadivinitymagazine.com

Fantasia Divinity Magazine

Table of Contents

MAGIC FOR BEGINNERS

Presented by Fantasia Divinity

DAMARA AND THE PIRATES

By Rebecca Buchanan

"That's it, Damara. Very good! Concentrate!"

Damara bit her lip and squinted at the phoenix that floated in the air above her head. Not that it was a real phoenix, of course. They only lived in the mountains far across the desert to the west. No, this was an illusion, a spell woven of color and light -- which was why the phoenix was a little blurry, its tail was too long, and, come to think of it, the phoenix' head feathers were the completely wrong color ....

Behind Damara, her grandfather tapped his staff against the floor in irritation. "Concentrate, child!"

Damara curled her hands into fists and squinted harder. She felt the magic curl around her like a warm wind. It wanted to do something, but it was resisting. Almost as if the magic wanted to help, but she was telling it the wrong thing to do ....

"Concen --"

With a whoosh and a warm poof, the phoenix exploded in a cloud of color and light. Tendrils of magic drifted through the air, settling for a moment on the floor and on her clothes and in her hair before they, too, evaporated.

Behind Damara, her grandfather sighed.

Blinking rapidly to hold back tears of frustration and disappointment, Damara slowly turned to face him.

Zalal the High Heka, the greatest wizard in all the land of Neilah, sat hunched in his chair. His knee-length kilt was a brilliant white, and numerous gold, red, and green rings covered his fingers. He held his serpent staff in one hand, the red jewels of its eyes seeming to glare at Damara. With his other hand, Zalal rubbed wearily at his shaved head.

He sighed again. "Well. That was ... better. You held the illusion for much longer today."

"Yes, Grandfather. Thank you, Grandfather," Damara whispered.

He cleared his throat, slapping one hand against his knee as he slowly stood. "Well, I must be off. The Great Council is meeting with the Phara. Important matters to discuss. We will try again tomorrow."

"Yes, Grandfather."

With that, he turned and left the room, his staff tap-tap-tapping against the floor.

Damara waited until he was gone to scrub the tears from her eyes. What was *wrong* with her? She could feel the magic around her. Sometimes she could even smell it: like cloves and cinnamon warmed by the sun. But she couldn't make it *work*. At least not for very long.

She wanted to scream in frustration. Or kick something really hard. Or just sit down and cry.

Instead, she climbed out the window.

***

The Great Pyramid of Neilah towered over the capital city. Fifty stories tall, made of creamy stone and capped in gold, it was filled with feasting halls and council rooms and bedchambers and shrines. Wide open doorways led to gardens filled with trees and flowers and birds. Half a dozen waterfalls cascaded down its sides, filling ponds and swimming pools before flowing away to join the Neilah River. From here, Phara Amenhasa III ruled all of Neilah, its cities and villages and farms spread up and down the river from the Triple Waterfall in the south to the Green Sea in the north.

And someday Prince Masa would rule after her.

Assuming he could stay awake through his lessons.

Damara peered over the edge of the patio wall. The outer stone of the pyramid had been smooth once, but centuries of sandstorms and wind had created small pits and grooves and cracks; more than enough handholds and footholds for her to get to wherever she wanted to go.

Damara narrowed her eyes. Beyond the bright sunlight, within the cool interior of the Prince's private classroom, she could see Scholar Anisi pacing back and forth in front of a large map of Neilah. Prince Masa slouched in a chair with his back to her, his legs thrown out, one arm dangling. His head was tipped to the side. If he wasn't asleep yet, he soon would be.

Anisi turned in his pacing, his voice a low drone. "... And so it was that Phara Setahasa, blessed be his name, invited the Cobras, the Jackals, the Lions, and the Falcons to take shelter with his people in their city by the lake. And all have lived in harmony and mutual support ever since ...."

Heerah lay on the stone floor beside the prince, tail twitching rhythmically, his fine mane dancing in the light breeze. The lion was close enough to leap to Masa's defense if necessary, but far enough away that the prince couldn't start weaving braids in his mane if he got *really* bored.

Damara stifled a giggle at the memory, but not quickly enough.

Heerah lifted his massive head, golden eyes fixing on her, his whole body still.

She lifted a hand over the wall of the patio and waved.

Heerah harrumphed and dropped his head back to the floor.

".... Such is not the case in the barbarian lands to the north, however," Anisi continued, "where Falcons are kept in bondage and the Cobras were hunted to extinction ...."

Masa snorted and jerked, mumbling something under his breath.

Damara shook her head. Definitely asleep. Perhaps they should switch places: she could study the history and customs of Neilah and he could study magic with her grandfather.

No.

Damara sighed and pulled herself up onto the wall of the balcony. Legs dangling, she turned to look out across the city towards the southern horizon. She had a responsibility to her grandfather, and her parents, and the grandmother she had never known, and every heka in her family who had come before her. She had magic. She did. She just --

"Damara!"

"Ah!' she shrieked, nearly sliding off the wall. Arms flailing, she grabbed blindly. There was nothing but air beneath her feet and she could see straight down the slope of the Pyramid to the ground far, far below --

Familiar hands closed around her wrists and sharp teeth caught the back of her dress. Carefully, Masa and Heerah pulled her back up and over the wall and onto the patio.

Panting, she slapped at Masa's hand. "Don't do that! Don't scare me like that!"

Masa grinned at her. "Sorry," he said, very clearly not sorry.

Damara tugged at her clothes, feeling for rips and tears. She felt only a wet spot on the back. "Thank you, Lord Heerah."

The Lion rumbled a low purr. "You are most welcome, Heka Damara. His highness should take more care: it is prey he needs to approach with stealth, not pridemates."

Masa's grin turned into a frown. "I wasn't being stealthy. She just didn't hear me. Too far inside her own head again." He turned back to Damara. "Are you done with your lessons? Did it work? Did you make the phoenix? I bet it was spectacular!"

"Yes. No. Well, sort of. Not really."

Damara bit the inside of her lip, tears threatening again.

"Oh. I'm sorry." Masa took her hand. "Want to go to the Looking Spot? You always feel better there."

Behind them, Scholar Anisi cleared his throat. "Your Highness, we have not yet finished your lessons --"

Masa waved his hand dismissively. "Yes, yes, we're all done."

Anisi scowled, nearly hissing in frustration. He bowed stiffly and stomped out of the room.

"You really should pay more attention to his lessons. You'll need to know all of this when you are Phara."

Masa shrugged. "I won't be Phara for many years. I have plenty of time to learn." He climbed up onto the wall of the patio, tugging her along behind him. "Come on. Race you to the Looking Spot!"

***

The stone was warm beneath her fingers, but not too hot. They scampered and clambered and jumped from one stone to the next, the wind tugging at their clothes. Heerah followed close behind, his claws digging in tight, his mane like a wild golden halo.

Damara's mother had first shown her the Looking Spot when she was eight, and home for a rare visit. Seeing how upset Damara was at having failed yet another magical lesson, Ushal had taken her hand and led her along the outside of the Pyramid to the roof of an old balcony; it was part of a bedroom that had not been used in years, likely even forgotten. From here, the whole of the capital city and the lake had spread out before them and, for a time, with her mother at her side, Damara had forgotten her sorrows.

It was a secret place that Damara had shared with no one except Masa and Heerah.

To reach the Looking Spot from Masa's private classroom, though, they had to pass the Phara's council chambers.

A small columned balcony extended out from the chamber. The two guards stationed there, tall spears in hand, shields at the ready, spotted them as soon as Damara, Masa and Heerah came into view. But Masa just waved an imperious hand. The guards looked at one another, looked back at Masa, and returned to attention.

Damara caught fragments of conversation as they climbed around the balcony, and risked a quick peek under the roof. She could see only a bit of the room and table and those who sat around it: Phara Amenhasa III, wearing a simple white dress and a plain golden circlet around her forehead, her thick black hair loose around her shoulders; Zalal, with his staff Rashani now in serpent form and curled around his shoulders, sound asleep; the Great Lion, Heerah's pridemother, her face scarred and one ear torn; the Great Jackal, panting slightly in the heat, his hide a glossy black; the Great Falcon atop a fine wooden perch, his feathers a mixture of red and brown and white; the Great Cobra, as long as a man was tall, her hood flipping open and shut in agitation; and others that Damara could hear but not see.

"... at least the third incident that was known of ...."

"... vile thieves!"

"... raiding nests ...."

" ... but where are they taking them, and why?"

"... detestable pirates ...."

Her curiosity piqued, Damara stopped and twisted around, trying to peer under the balcony's roof again. But Masa grabbed her hand and Heerah pushed his nose into her chest, forcing her upright.

"This is not for the ears of children, Heka. If they wish you to know of it, the Phara or your grandfather will tell you."

"Oh, I --"

"Come on!" Masa tugged harder on her hand.

Relenting, Damara followed him the rest of the way to the Looking Spot.

Their small stash of supplies was still there, undisturbed. Masa unrolled the blanket and spread it across the balcony's roof while Damara opened the leather satchel and pulled out a pouch of water, pieces of flat bread, and a small bag of honey candy.

For long minutes, they sat in silence, enjoying the treats. The wind danced around them. Falcons and hawks and ravens whirled through the air. Below them, a waterfall tumbled down the side of the pyramid to fill a swimming pool, then split and fell again to a reflecting pool far down at the bottom. Beyond that lay the city of Neilah itself, the houses of mud and wood painted a white so bright that it hurt Damara's eyes. Colorful geometric patterns rimmed their doors and windows. The lake was deep blue, the wind carrying tiny fishing vessels and larger cargo ships across its surface and onto the river. Far, far in the distance, across the arid desert, Damara could just make out the shadows of the mountains where phoenixes made their nests.

And where her mother was now, watching the border, using her magic to protect Neilah.

"I will never be High Heka," she whispered.

Masa shifted closer, licking the honey off his fingers. "Do you *want* to be High Heka?"

"I ...." Damara frowned. "I don't know. I want to be a heka. I *am* a heka. I have magic. I just can't make it work right."

"I don't care if you never get your magic to work right."

Damara flinched. "What?"

"I mean. Well, it's just, you're my friend. You've *always* been my friend and you always will be. You'll still be my friend after I am crowned Phara. And, well, I'll need you. 'Cause I don't think I'll like being Phara. It's all memorizing harvest figures and making trade deals and signing treaties and listening to people talk, talk, talk. It's so *boring*. I want to be out there, like your mother is, not stuck in the pyramid all day ...." Masa grimaced. "Sorry. I was trying to make you feel better, and just ended up complaining and talking about myself. What I meant to say was that you'll always be my friend, no matter what. If you're High Heka, a regular heka, or ... or ... a candy-seller in the market. It won't matter to me."

Beside them, Heerah rumbled in approval, his face turned towards the sun.

Damara felt a small smile curl the corners of her lips as a bit -- just a bit -- of the frustration and anger lifted away. She was still a disappointment to her grandfather and her mother and herself. But at least she could never be a disappointment to Masa.

She held up the empty bag. "More honey candy?"

Masa grinned and jumped to his feet.

***

In late afternoon, the central market of Neilah was crowded with shoppers, merchants, poets, fortune tellers, and city guard. Humans, Jackals, Lions, and Cobras all mingled together, filling the plaza with laughter, shouts, growls, and howls. Falcons winged overhead, occasionally diving down to roost atop the colorful stalls. Poets stood on stone pedestals, reciting ancient epics and tales of wily wizards. And the city guard prowled, ever on alert, the humans with their swords and the Jackals with their ears perked.

Damara and Masa wandered for hours, Heerah only a step behind. They bought and ate an entire bag of honey candy. They had yellow flowers painted on their cheeks and danced to the music of drums and flutes. They stopped to see a fortune teller, who sat in the shadow of a dozing Cobra, its hood extended to protect her from the sun.

The fortune teller hmmed and hummed, peered at their palms, and squinted at their teeth. Peering at Masa, she calmly announced, "Your heart is closed. It shall be pierced open."

Masa frowned. "What does that mean?"

But the fortune teller just dropped his hands and turned to Damara. "Do not sleep! Do not close your eyes! Danger sails before you!"

Damara felt a shiver spread up her arms. "I -- I will. I mean, I won't."

Masa snorted and scrambled to his feet. "Come on. I heard there are acrobats performing in front of the temple of Bezh."

Casting one last glance over her shoulder at the fortune teller, Damara followed him into the crowd, Heerah close to her side.

***

The acrobats were accompanied by mimes, fire-breathers, and sword-swallowers. Masa pulled Damara from one amazing feat to the next, whooping and cheering. Damara held her breath at the sight of the Falcon who caught arrows in mid-air, and shrieked in awe at the Lion who could roar fire.

Only when a cool breeze blew in off the lake and tangled in her hair did she realize how long they had spent in the market. Looking up in surprise, she saw that the sun was on the western horizon and the sky above was shading from bright blue to deep purple. Torches had been lit and the market was beginning to empty as the shops closed and people made their way home for the evening meal.

Masa threw up his hands in disappointment when the acrobats offered one last bow and then began to pack away their swords and balls and hoops.

"Phooey," he muttered.

Damara bumped his shoulder sympathetically. "We should return to the pyramid, anyway."

"Come along, cublings. You have been filling your bellies with sweets all day." Heerah nodded his big head at the pyramid which loomed above the city, its cap glowing with a magical golden light. "It is time for a real dinner, and then bed. You have studies to continue tomorrow."

With that, Damara felt her stomach tighten with anxiety again. Her feet dragging, she followed Heerah and Masa through the winding streets. The wind rose again, pulling at her dress and hair, and the sky darkened. Magical torches sprang to life, casting just enough light for them to see, and, in the distance, Damara could hear city guard on patrol, their swords rattling.

A flash of shadow overhead. Damara stopped and tilted her head back, watching as a sharp-winged Falcon crossed the crescent of the moon. Back and forth.

She frowned. That was odd. Falcons were creatures of the day. Strange for one to be about now, after sunset, unless it had urgent --

A shout. A cry of alarm and outrage.

Looking around, Damara suddenly realized that she was alone.

Where was Masa? Where was Heerah?

Another shout, and frantic barking.

Damara ran towards the sound, sandals digging into the stone street. Around one corner and another, trying to find the shout again, and she was yelling herself, calling "Masa! Heerah! Masa! Where are you?"

Around another corner, pebbles skidding beneath her feet. She almost fell, caught the wall with her hand to keep herself upright. There. Down the street -- a narrow alley, really -- Masa with Heerah in front of him, teeth bared in a fierce snarl, and two men that Damara did not recognize. They had a cart with a cage inside and – oh dear, oh no – there were Jackal pups and Lion cubs in the cage and they were --

One of the men lifted his staff, swinging it out in a wide arc. He whispered a spell, the words slippery and soft. Heka spread out from the tip of the staff like a green blanket, covering the alley. It settled on Masa and Heerah and reached out towards Damara. She caught its scent: strange trees and cold earth.

She scrambled backwards, trying to escape, watching in horror as Masa and Heerah collapsed to the ground.

The magic caught her and she blinked rapidly, fighting the urge to lay down and sleep. Her feet tangled, feeling heavy, and she fell, banging her elbows against the stone. She blinked again, calling up her magic, calling her heka to help her. She could feel it, smell it, warm and golden ....

Bits of conversation penetrated the green haze of sleep.

"... leave the Lion, grab the boy!"

"What?"

"... too heavy. The boy saw us!"

"Hurry!"

"-- city guard --"

Damara dragged herself around, her head fuzzy, trying to focus on the strange men. Her breath caught in her chest. They were taking him! They were taking Masa!

Damara struggled to keep her eyes open, watching as they tossed Masa into the cage with the pups and cubs. The man with the staff slammed the door closed and locked the cage. He glanced around, then up as a Falcon swooped down into the alley.

For a moment, Damara almost laughed in relief.

But then she saw the leather straps hanging from the Falcon's legs, and saw it settle on the man's arm, and she realized that this Falcon was no friend.

The cart lurched forward and disappeared around a corner, the two strange men following, and Damara dropped her head as sleep finally claimed her.

***

She dreamt of her mother and her grandfather and honey candy and phoenixes with their brilliant red tails and Masa, laughing at the acrobats --

With a cry, Damara lurched upright. Her legs still heavy and awkward, she struggled to stand. Looking around, she spotted Heerah, his eyes closed, his jaws wide as he snored.

Stumbling, she made her way down the alley and fell against his side. She shoved at him, yelled his name, tugged his ears. But he continued to snore.

Damara slumped against the Lion and cried.

Masa was gone.

Her magic was useless. *Useless.*

What was the point of having heka if she couldn't protect her best friend?

... But it had protected her against the sleep spell, at least a little .... She glanced up at the moon, noting that it was almost in the same position. She hadn't slept for very long.

Maybe her heka wasn't so useless, after all.

Biting her lip, she lifted her hands and concentrated. She drew the shape of a phoenix in the air, building the image in her mind: the long tail feathers, the wide wings, the sharp beak and shining eyes.

Her magic responded, gathering around her. Gradually, it took the shape she wanted, fuzzy at first, but then more distinct. Her magic coalesced, took form, and a soft golden phoenix appeared before her eyes.

It was small, not much bigger than her hand, and its gentle glow warmed her skin.

The phoenix trilled, and Damara laughed in relief.

Pressing her hands to Heerah's side, she pushed herself to her feet. "Find Masa," she told the phoenix. "Take me to Masa."

The phoenix spun in a slow circle, gliding on a wind that she could not feel. Trilling again, it turned sharply and flew down the alley.

"Wait for me!" Damara yelled, and followed the tiny bird into the night.

***

Up one street and down another, passed shuttered stores and darkened temples and quiet homes. The moon climbed higher in the sky, and the scents and sounds of the lake grew stronger: the smell of fish and wet earth, the brush of wind across water, the low slap of waves against wooden hulls and wooden docks.

Damara ran while the phoenix twirled and whirled ahead of her, spinning in slow circles, diving high and then plummeting back towards the street.

And then suddenly the street ended and they were at the docks, great wooden tongues stretching out into the lake. Ships of all shapes and sizes bobbed gently in the water, some flat barges, some cargo vessels, some pleasure crafts with beautifully painted hulls and colorful sails. The docks spread up and down the shore of the lake, illuminated by magical torches whose light cast strange shadows and reflections in the water.

Damara stumbled to a halt and crouched behind a pile of crates and nets. The dock directly in front of her was some fifty feet long, with a dozen vessels tied up on either side. Most of the ships sat silent; it would be hours yet before the fishermen rose from their beds. But there was movement on a handful of vessels, shadows striding back and forth as sailors moved cargo around and repaired nets and sails by lantern light.

How was she --

Damara hissed when she realized that the phoenix was still gliding along, trilling happily. Stretching its wings, the bird arced up through the air and settled atop the mast of one ship far down on the right side of the dock, its sides draped with nets and ropes, a wide cabin of painted wood and fine fabrics near the stern.

"Go away!" Damara whispered, her voice hoarse. "Go away or someone will see you!"

The phoenix cocked its head at her. Slowly, its soft golden glow faded until, with a flicker, it vanished completely.

For a long minute, Damara held her breath, waiting for an alarm to sound.

Nothing.

Crawling on her hands and knees, she made her way around the crates, moving from one hiding spot to the next. The wind off the lake tugged at her hair and dress. The ground scraped her hands and knees.

And then she ran out of places to hide.

Peering around a broken cart and a stack of broken anchor stones and shredded ropes, she squinted down the length of the dock. The ship where Masa was being held was still some thirty feet away. She could just make out the shadow of a man wandering back and forth across the deck. A guard. She would certainly be seen if she walked straight down the dock.

Perhaps she could swim --

A fierce, angry roar echoed through the streets behind her. The sound made her heart thud in fear and her stomach twist.

Heerah. The Lion had awakened and was calling for the city guard.

Damara felt herself smiling in relief. Between Heerah and the Jackals of the city guard, they would easily track Masa to the ship. The guard would arrive soon, arrest the kidnappers, and free Masa and the cubs and pups who had been taken.

Her smile disappeared when, with a loud crash and a shouted curse, the man with the staff came out of the cabin. The Falcon wobbled on his shoulder, wings partially extended for balance. Scowling, the man leaned over the railing of the ship, towards the city.

Heerah let loose another angry roar.

The man turned, waving his staff as more crew surged onto the deck. "Cast off, cast off!" he shouted. "The stupid Lion is awake already!"

No no nonono.

Damara scuttled out from behind the broken cart.

They were leaving! The city guard would never arrive in time. The ship would be far out on the lake and heading into the river. It would quickly become lost among the hundreds of other ships making their way up and down the waterway -- and Damara had no doubt that the man with the staff would use his heka to disguise the ship.

She would never see Masa again.

Scrambling back behind the cart, she lifted her hands and whispered low under her breath. Her magic responded, gathering around her. She felt it draw in close, settling around her like a cloak. Her hands faded, and then her arms, and when she looked down, she could no longer see her feet or legs.

She tossed aside her sandals. Bent low, her steps quick, she made her way down the dock.

A pair of sailors -- no, not sailors; *pirates* -- jumped down and began tugging at the ropes that held the ship in place. On the ship, two other pirates lifted long, stout poles which they jammed against the dock. The ship started to move away.

One of the pirates darted over towards Damara, scrambling to unknot the rope as it began to pull tight.

She froze. She was close enough to see the dirt under his fingernails and the holes in his sandals. Holding her breath, biting her lip, Damara started to tiptoe passed him. She froze again when he turned and jumped back onto the ship, the second pirate quickly following.

The ship was moving away from the dock. It was already too far for her to jump safely.

Hissing under her breath, Damara sat down on the dock, dangling her legs over the edge. Twisting around, she gingerly lowered herself into the cool water of the lake. Something brushed past her leg, and she told herself that it was just a fish or turtle. Not a crocodile.

Kicking hard, invisible arms out-stretched, she reached for the ship. Not quite. Another kick, and another. The flower on her cheek dribbled paint. The ship was beginning to swing around, the bow pointing out towards the open water.

Nearly crying in frustration, Damara kicked again and again. As the fat stern of the ship came around, she made one last mad grab -- and caught the dangling edge of a net. She curled her fingers tight, clinging to the net as the sails overhead lowered and snapped into place. She could hear the man with the staff again, not shouting, but snapping at the crew to "hurry, hurry!"

Lifting her other arm, Damara hauled herself higher onto the net. Grunting as the fibers bit into her skin, she kicked up with one invisible leg and managed to snag the net with her toes. Second leg, kick. There.

Damara hung on the net for long moments, panting, trying to catch her breath.

Water dribbled into her eyes. Shaking her head, she slowly climbed up the net. When her fingers touched the railing, she hesitated. Straining, she could only hear the scuffling of feet and the snap of the sails. She cautiously lifted her head, peering onto the deck of the ship.

Two hatches, one fore and one aft, led into the belly of the ship. Half a dozen pirates moved about, tightening ropes and watching for obstructions in the water; a few cast wary glances at the dock as it fell away behind them. The man with the staff was nowhere to be seen; perhaps he was inside the cabin again.

Damara hauled herself onto the railing. Her foot dangled, her hand slipped, and she went sprawling across the deck. She pushed herself up against the side, scrambling out of the way just as a pirate ran passed her.

With one more quick look around, she crawled across the deck towards the aft hatch. Squinting into the darkness below, she caught a whiff of wet wood, straw, beer, and other things she couldn't name. Drawing a deep breath, she slid her legs around and carefully climbed down the steep stairs.

A single magical lantern illuminated the cargo hold, which took up the entire back end of the ship. It was filled floor to ceiling with crates, vases, bags -- and cages.

Jackal pups. Lion cubs. Eggs tucked into straw nests: tiny speckled Falcon eggs and glossy black Cobra eggs. Dozens of them. Most of the pups and cubs were asleep. A few blinked at her in confusion. Their fur was matted and dirty.

Damara gaped at the sight. For a long moment, she could only stare in horror.

And then the anger came. Fury boiled up through her belly, heating her neck and face. Her chest tightened and she felt her heka respond. Her magic got hot, turning in a flash from warm and comforting to blistering.

"Damara?"

The voice was slurred and sleepy. Peering around, Damara finally spied Masa. He lay in a cage towards the back of the cargo hold, high up on a stack of boxes.

"Masa!" she whispered, voice hoarse. She scrambled across the hold, moving around bags and crates. When she reached him, she had to crane her neck back to see --

"Wait, you can see me?"

Masa blinked and frowned in confusion. "'Course I can see you. Why'nt?"

Damara lifted her hands. Her visible hands.

"Wha hap'n?"

"Pirates!" Damara pulled herself onto her tiptoes, trying to see him better. "I think these are the people that your mother and the council were talking about."

"Uh?" Masa blinked again, his gaze still unfocused, his body limp.

"The -- never mind. I have to get you out of that cage. We have to get off this ship before they get too far from shore." She shivered at the thought of having to swim back through the lake, crocodiles lurking in the water below.

Damara looked around, hunting for a nail or a hammer or bar or something she could use to open the cage.

"Keez," Masa slurred. He waggled a finger towards the hatch.

She turned and there, on the edge of the doorframe, hung the keys, swinging slightly as the ship bobbed in the water.

Dodging across the hold, she snatched the keys off their hook and sprinted back to Masa. She nearly tripped over a bag of wheat and her elbow banged into a cage filled with Cobra eggs. She flinched, hoping that no one had heard the sound and that she hadn't damaged any of the eggs. Scrabbling around, she found a nearly empty box and dragged it across the floor. She quickly hopped on top of it and shoved a key into the lock of Masa's cage. The two Jackal pups that lay beside him snored softly. One of the Lion cubs was slumped across Masa's legs, while another blinked at her and mewled, his ears flattened in distress.

Again, she felt that boil of magic across her skin.

Wrong key. She tried another. And another.

Masa half-lifted his head. "Behin' you!"

Damara started to turn. Strong arms clamped hard around her waist, lifting her high into the air. Damara shrieked, kicking, trying to pull her arms free. She smelled fish and beer as an angry voice snarled in her ear, "Knew we had a stowaway! Think you're so clever! Didn't think we'd see the water you left all over the deck?"

Damara kicked again, swinging her foot back, trying to find his knee. She felt her heka pull in tight around her, sliding across her skin, uncertain, waiting for her to tell it what to do.

"Let go!" she screamed. "Let go!"

A phoenix burst into existence, its light filling the hold. The bird was massive, easily the size of a Lion. Wings covered in gold and red feathers spread wide, and its great golden beak opened in a loud screech. Flinging its head back, tail feathers snapping, it disappeared up through the ceiling.

The pirate dropped Damara, stumbled backwards, and fled back up the steps. She landed funny, banging her elbows again, and dropped the keys.

Above, more shouting and the sounds of running feet. Damara recognized one voice: the man with the staff. "You fools! They've seen us! The phoenix!" His voice, heavy with fear and anger, drew closer, and then he was at the hatch, thudding down the stairs. He gripped his staff tightly in one hand and his eyes, when they landed on Damara, were cold with hate. "You miserable little -- "

Damara shouted in surprise as the ship suddenly lurched to a stop. There was a terrible grinding, rending sound. Wood groaned. Bags and vases tipped over. Crates and cages tumbled. The man with the staff crashed to the floor, banging his head on a clay vase.

"Masa! Masa, are you hurt?" Damara climbed to her knees, frantically feeling around for the keys. Wheat, more wheat, broken vase of wine, rope. Something dull glittered under a broken box. Shoving it aside, she pulled out the keyring. "Masa?"

"I'm ... I'm all right. Damara, where are you?"

"I'm coming! Just hold on!" Scrambling over and around more crates and cages, feet slipping on ripped bags of wheat, Damara made her way through the mess of the hold. Some of the cubs and pups had awakened, and they whimpered and barked, scratching at their cages. A Falcon egg rolled against her ankle, and she narrowly missed stepping on it.

Overhead, the shouting grew louder and more desperate. Light poured down through the hatch, and she could hear snarls and roars and the clang of swords and shields.

She finally reached Masa. His cage was on its side, the locked door facing up. He held the two sleeping Jackal pups against his chest, while the Lions pressed against his legs and mewled. His skirt was torn and stained, and there was wheat in his hair.

"Almost -- just a moment." Damara jammed a key into the lock, then another. The third fit. Twisting it, she heaved the door open.

Masa stood and handed her the two Jackal pups. Leaning back down, he picked up the Lions, then swung his leg through the door. "We have to free the others."

Damara shook her head. "Not yet. I think Heerah is here. Come on. Be careful where you step. There are eggs everywhere."

The man with the staff groaned as they moved around him and cautiously made their way up the steps.

The deck swarmed with pirates, city guard, Lions, and Jackals. A pair of Falcons screamed overhead, claws extended and wings batting one another. Zalal stood on the far end of the ship, his staff half-transformed so that the snake's head whipped back and forth, snapping and hissing. Zalal's eyes widened when he saw her, and he took a step forward.

"Grandfather!" Damara shouted. She was out of the hatch and halfway across the deck when he suddenly lifted his staff and threw it at her.

No. Not at her.

The snake shifted in midair, flying over her head, eyes flashing.

She turned just in time to see the snake wrap around the man with the staff. Round and round it twisted its long body, mouth wide, fangs glistening. The man stumbled, arms and legs bound tight. His staff clattered to the deck and he fell, gasping for air.

"Take care, Rashani." Zalal came up beside Damara, his hand settling on her shoulder. He glared down at the man, whose face had turned purple. "We have many questions to ask him. Best just to keep him still until the guard can take him into custody."

The snake hissed in annoyance, but loosened its coils. The man gurgled and slumped, his eyes still cold and angry.

Zalal knelt down in front of Damara. Around them, the fighting slowed and then ceased as the last of the pirates surrendered. Jackals snarled. The tethered Falcon dropped to the deck, one of its wings bleeding; a city guard caught the bird in a blanket, holding it close to keep it from escaping. Heerah bounded across the deck, swiped her face with his big tongue (cleaning away the last of the yellow flower), and then nearly pounced on Masa. The prince giggled as the Lion ran his tongue all over the boy's face and hair.

"I must apologize, Granddaughter."

Damara frowned up at Zalal. "What? Why?"

"Your heka. I ... misunderstood it. I thought your magic was like mine and Ushal's. But it is not. Your heka is meant to protect. That is why none of my lessons were effective. That is why your heka never really worked before, but did here." He waved one hand around. The city guard had already gathered up the pirates and were leading them down the plank towards ... oh. A muddy path led away from the ship, straight back to the shore.

"You called up the bottom of the lake!" Damara blurted. "That's why the ship stopped! You created a sandbar."

Zalal smiled and nodded. "Yes. But I was only able to do so because *you* showed us which ship had carried you away. I'm sure that your phoenix was visible all the way across the city in the Great Pyramid itself."

Damara felt a blush heating her cheeks.

"From now on, your lessons will be very different. I am also most curious to know how you found this ship in the first place, and how you managed to get on board."

"She made herself invisible!" Masa crowed. He was still hugging the two Lion cubs, who had stopped mewling once Heerah began to lick them, too.

Zalal frowned at the prince. "Your mother will have words for you when we return."

Masa opened his mouth as if to protest. But slowly his expression changed. He looked down at the deck for a moment. Then he straightened his shoulders and walked over to them. Heerah followed, pressed tight against his side.

"You are correct, High Heka. And mother *should* have words for me. I acted irresponsibly and put Damara and Heerah in danger." The Lion snorted, but Masa continued. "I didn't know. I didn't know about the pirates, or that some Falcons live as slaves and serve men. I didn't know that such men could be a danger to Neilah or its people." His gaze dropped to the cubs for a moment. "All of its people."

When he looked up at Damara, his expression was solemn. "I meant what I said at the Looking Spot. I'll always be your friend, no matter what. But I am glad that you found your magic."

Damara started to answer, but Masa shook his head and continued, "I will be Phara someday. When I am, will you help me protect our people?"

"I will," she promised, and it was a promise that she would keep.

About the Author

Rebecca Buchanan is the editor of the Pagan literary ezine, Eternal Haunted Summer. She has been published in a variety of venues, including Abyss and Apex, Enchanted Conversation, Haunted House (Flame Tree Publishing), Mirror Dance, and The Society of Misfit Stories, among others.

THE MAGIC FORK

By Liam Martin

Megan waved her wand at the vase of lilies again, but nothing happened that time either. What was she doing wrong? Callum had already managed to turn his sunflowers into a bunch of bananas, Becky had transformed her daisies into a baseball, even Sophie had been able to make her dandelions go a bit green.

Ever since Megan had moved to middle school and started doing actual magic she had struggled. It was like something was holding her back, she always kept wondering 'am I doing this the right way?' or 'am I saying the spell right?.' Before that she was top in the class across the board. She just loved to read and learn new things. Ms. Willow even said she was the brightest witch they had seen at Magibrook Elementary School in a long time.

"So how are you doing?" Mrs. Eldritch asked, stooping over Megan's table.

"I just cannot seem to make the spell work," she told her.

Mrs. Eldritch pursed her lips, "I trust you remember how to do it."

"Yes, Mrs, first you make the picture in your mind of the thing you want the flowers to turn into, and then you shut your eyes tight, say the magic words, and wave your wand."

"Very good, Megan, that was word-for-word the instructions I gave you at the start of class, it shows that you are a very keen listener. Now let us try casting the spell again."

"Ok, Mrs."

She began to picture one of the radishes her grandad grew in his garden. She thought about them so hard that she even started to smell them.

Then she shut her eyes, said the magic words, and flicked her wand.

But nothing happened.

"Not to worry," Mrs. Eldritch said leaning in closer towards her so that none of the other children could overhear, "I have another idea." She took a fork out of the pocket of her robe. "See this fork, this is a magic fork."

"Are you sure, because it looks like the forks from the cafeteria," Megan said.

"You can't get a fork like this from a cafeteria, it is very ancient and very powerful. It channels a person's magical energy and amplifies their spells. All the best witches and wizards have one, you know. Maybe it will help you," she handed the fork to her. "Take it."

Megan took it and put it in her pocket. She did not really believe it, it seemed silly. If it was a ring or a crystal, she might have believed it, but a fork?

"Now give it another try," Mrs. Eldritch said. The way she looked at Megan, with big, hopeful eyes made her feel like she would be letting her down if she did not take it seriously, so Megan tried the spell again.

She thought of radishes like last time. Then she shut her eyes and said the magic words. And then…

It worked.

When she opened her eyes there was a big red radish peeking over the top of the vase.

She did it!

"Not bad, Megan," Callum said.

She blushed. "Thanks," she answered.

"So how come it worked this time and not all of the times before?" he asked.

"I don't know, I guess I must have just got lucky," she told him, winking at Mrs. Eldritch.

After class, Megan went up to Mrs. Eldritch and tried to give her the fork back. "No, you keep it," she said.

"Are you sure, Mrs?" Megan asked.

"I am, just do not tell anyone that it was me who gave it to you."

"Thank you," Megan said putting the fork back into her pocket.

The rest of the day seemed to whizz by. Megan was making the most of her newly-found magical ability. In herbalism class she turned a parsley leaf into a grasshopper, in divination she turned a teapot from china to gold, and in runology she rearranged the runes in a hundred-year-old spell book to say 'megz woz ere.'

At the end of the day, when she was just about to step out of the school gates, the headmaster called to her.

Mr. Hocus was very strict and proper, the type of headmaster that preferred his pupils to be seen and not heard. He had neatly combed black hair and a pencil moustache.

"Miss Megan, is that a fork in your pocket?" he asked.

Megan looked down. The fork was sticking out of her pocket. "It is, sir," she said.

"And why is there a fork in your pocket?"

"It is not just any fork, sir, it is a magic fork."

"A magic fork," he said stroking his chin, "and who gave you this magic fork?"

"Sorry, sir, I cannot tell you."

"Was it Mrs. Eldritch by any chance?" Mr. Hocus guessed.

Megan's face whitened and her eyes widened.

"I thought so. For some reason Mrs. Eldritch has taken it upon herself to take ordinary forks from the cafeteria and give them to students, telling them they are magic. She has this silly idea in her head that it makes the student stop doubting themselves and believe in their own ability," he said. "So, can I have my fork back?"

Megan took the fork from her pocket and handed it to Mr. Hocus, but not before she had silently cast an animation spell on it.

As soon as the headmaster took the fork, it sprouted two tiny legs. It leapt from his hands and began running around the courtyard.

"Come back here this instant!" Mr. Hocus shouted, chasing after it.

Megan ran out of the school gates, and then all the way home.

She never struggled to cast a spell again.

About the Author

Liam Martin is a writer from Nottinghamshire in the United Kingdom. He has a BA in Creative Writing from the University of Derby and is currently studying a MA in English Studies at the University of Nottingham.

MOLLIE'S MAGIC BOOK

By Margaret Bailes

It was a book about magic. Card tricks and rope tricks and the classic finding a coin behind the ear trick. It came with a wand, not just a cheap plastic one but polished timber which felt heavy and well balanced in your hand.

Mollie liked the wand best, but thanked Aunt Hannah for the gift of the book. "I expect to see a magic show next time I come to visit," Aunt Hannah told her.

Mollie flipped through the book in bed that night and swished the wand and said "Abracadabra," as the book suggested. The book slid from her lap and as it landed on the floor, the dust cover slipped off. Mollie jumped out of bed to retrieve the book. As she folded back the flap of the dustcover, she noticed something written in small letters at the very bottom of the page.

She held the cover close to the bed lamp to make out what it was. There was a single word, Aperio. "Aperio," read Mollie. Now that sounded like a real magic word she thought, much better than abracadabra. She tucked the book back into the dust cover and placed it on the bedside table with the wand placed on top. She fell asleep wondering what 'Aperio' meant.

Next morning Mollie woke early, it was Saturday and she didn't have to go to school. She took the book and wand and crept out of her bedroom to the kitchen where she prepared herself a bowl of cereal.

Sitting at the table, she opened the book and lifted the flap at the front. 'Aperio' was written there just as she remembered. Curious, she closed the book and turned over the flap at the back of the book. There was written another word, 'Absconditum'. It was a tongue twister and took Mollie a bit of practice to pronounce it correctly.

She waved her wand and said "Absconditum" in a deep, wizard like voice and then "Aperio!" She put the wand down on the book to take another spoon of cereal, but something made her stop mid chew on her cornflakes. The book had moved! It had shuddered as if there had been a mini earthquake, yet the table hadn't moved.

Mollie looked more closely at the book and turned the pages over. What she saw made her swallow her cornflakes in one big gulp. The pages didn't look like they had before. Instead of 'The Disappearing Knot Trick' there was a spell for invisibility, hand written in black scrawly writing on pages that were yellowed and old looking.

"Aperio!" repeated Mollie a little tentatively. Nothing happened. The book remained unmoved on the table open to the page titled 'Invisibility.' Mollie picked up the wand and pointed it at the book. She tried again. "Absconditum." The book suddenly shuddered and snapped shut. "Whoa!" croaked Mollie. She opened the book and saw the familiar pages of 'The Children's Book of Magic Tricks.' She pointed the wand at the book. "Aperio," she said excitedly. The book did its quick-change act and was an old spell book once more. "I can do magic!" she breathed.

She began reading the spell for invisibility and although it was a little difficult to make out some of the writing, there it was, the magic word to make someone invisible. Mollie held on tight to the wand and swished it around in the air to point it at herself saying at the same time, "Inobservatus."

She dropped the wand in surprise when she saw it floating in mid-air. She waved her hand about, she could feel her hand but not see it, she really had made herself invisible! But what she hadn't noticed was that at the same time she spoke the magic word and waved her wand, her parents had just walked into the kitchen, bleary eyed and looking for their morning cup of coffee.

Her mother's voice startled her. "I've told Mollie to pack away her dirty dishes into the dishwasher," she scolded. "She's just left it here on the table." Mollie watched in horror as her bowl suddenly levitated and floated towards the dishwasher. The door opened seemingly of its own accord and the bowl nestled into the rack. On the other side of the room a cupboard door opened, and two coffee mugs swooped down to rest on the bench top. Mollie heard her father yawn and rub his hand on his unshaven bristly face.

Oh no, I've made Mum and Dad invisible too, she realised.

As her parents were on opposite sides of the room with their backs to each other, they hadn't noticed that the other had been turned invisible. They obviously hadn't noticed their own invisibility yet either. Mollie had to change them back quickly.

Taking up the book and wand, she dashed to the door as a jar of coffee descended to sit beside the mug and the door of the dishwasher closed with a bang. She heard the beeping of the dishwasher button being pushed and the rattle of cutlery in the drawer.

She scanned the page, there had to be a word to change back! She should have read the whole thing before making the spell. Oh, why hadn't she thought to find the spell to end the spell! "Visabilis! It's visabilis!" she cried out loud, waving the wand desperately.

Her parents reappeared just as her Dad turned to say, "Coffee dear?"

Mollie's Mum looked around from the dishwasher. "Ooh, yes please." She noticed Mollie standing in the doorway. "Oh, there you are Mollie, did you just say something?"

"No Mum, I was just reading my new book," Mollie replied.

"Well," said Mum, 'Aunt Hannah will be pleased you like her gift, but you still need to do your chores, have you fed Max?'

"Not yet," admitted Mollie.

She wandered out on to the back deck, placing her book and wand on a chair before taking up a box of dog biscuits and giving it a shake. "C'mon Max!" she called. "Breakfast time." A tan and white Jack Russell scampered around the deck with his pointy tail wagging. Mollie rattled biscuits into his bowl. "Sit, Max," she told him firmly. Max sat obediently waiting for her to say it was OK to eat. Mollie watched as he gobbled up his biscuits. Now here was a good subject to practice the invisibility spell on.

Mollie took hold of the wand and at the magic word, Max disappeared. Mollie laughed to see dog biscuits also disappearing into thin air. Max crunched two last biscuits and it became very quiet.

"Max! Max!" Mollie called. "Max, where are you?" She walked around the side of the house and called again, listening for a bark or doggy panting, the patter of his paws on the path. She couldn't hear anything that might sound like an invisible dog. "Oh no, how can I turn you back if I can't find you, Max!" she cried.

Mollie swung her wand and called out, "Visabilis!" She turned and waved the wand in the other direction and said the magic word again. There was no sign of Max. She ran around the back yard waving the wand frantically and crying, "Visabilis! Visabilis!"

Her mother saw her from the kitchen window and called out, "Mollie, what are you doing?"

Mollie stopped mid wave of the wand. "Um, I'm just practicing my wand skills."

"Well, can you please come inside and get dressed," her Mum asked. "I thought we might take Max for a walk to the park."

Mollie felt herself begin to panic. How could she explain not being able to find Max? She had to find him. Mum would be looking for him soon to take him for his walk. Max loved going for walks. She had an idea.

"Max," she called again. "Do you want to go for a walk?" There was a sudden delighted yelp from Max and Mollie fell backwards on the grass as an excited Max jumped up on her. Mollie reached out to take hold of the squirming, licking dog. "Stay still Max," she laughed. "Visabilis!" Max wriggled free and ran to the back door where he leapt up and down.

Mollie was very relieved. That was two close calls. She decided that before she tried any more magic, she would take the time to read through the spell first. That made her think of what her teacher, Mrs. Johnson was always telling her. "You are a smart girl Mollie, you just need to take your time and think things through, don't rush." It really was good advice, so Mollie sat up in bed that evening and methodically went through the magic book reading each of the spells in it.

She read through spells for super strength and super speed. They sounded like fun, she thought. Being able to walk through walls could come in handy, so could changing the weather. Two spells, however, sounded exciting, the spell of flight and the spell for shape shifting. There were magic spells for transforming into all kinds of animals. Mollie thought that she would try the spell for transforming into a cat, just for a few minutes to see what it would be like.

She sat up on the bed and taking her wand, said the magic words, "Transformo Felis Catus!" The room seemed to grow bigger around her, the bed stretched out long and wide, but it was Mollie who had shrunk. She looked down to see two ginger paws and realised she was standing on all fours and had a long swishing tail. She tentatively jumped down on to the floor and was amazed at how easily and gracefully her cat body moved.

She tensed and sprang up onto the chest of drawers landing easily on top. She stared in surprise at her reflection in the mirror, a long lithe ginger striped body and big green eyes that looked back in wonder. A breeze blew the curtain at the window and Mollie the cat turned her head to look out at the garden. Did she dare go outdoors? It was a lovely summer night with a large moon shining in the sky. Without a second thought, Mollie jumped onto the window sill and out into the night.

Mollie ran across the back lawn. It felt strange to walk on all fours, but she felt strong and agile. She was enjoying being a cat prowling around the yard. A sudden loud, furious barking made her fur stand up in fright. Max had just discovered a strange cat in his territory. He ran towards her, larger than life with his teeth bared. Mollie turned and ran for the tree by the fence, Max right behind her. With her claws extended, she sprang up the tree, climbing until she reached a branch out of Max's reach. Her heart was pounding. Max continued to sound the alarm and it wasn't long before Mollie heard her father's annoyed shout, "Max! come here, Max!"

Max gave a final defiant bark at the intruder in the tree and reluctantly returned to the house. "Bad boy Max, go to bed!" Mollie heard her father say. Peeking through the leaves, she saw her Dad return inside and Max crawl into his bed, turning in a circle before plonking down with a resigned sigh. She thought it might be best to go back to her room, and back to being her own self. She looked for a safe route to her window, not wanting to run across the lawn again and risk Max seeing her.

Jumping lightly from the branch to the top of the fence, she carefully made her way around to the side of the house. Quickly, she bounced down then up onto the window sill and the safety of her room. Only when she was back on her bed with the book open in front of her did she wonder how she was to turn back into herself. Could she still speak, or would she miaow like a cat? How would she use the wand with paws instead of hands?

Mollie closed her eyes and said in a tiny, hopeful voice, "Reverti." She was very relieved to hear her own voice say it, and even more so when she felt her body stretch out upon the bed. She wiggled her fingers in front of her face and breathed a big sigh of relief. The spell had worked, and it had worked without the wand. This made Mollie wonder if the other spells would work without the wand as well?

She tried it out. "Inobservatus," she said. She looked down, her legs sticking out of her striped pyjama shorts were still very visible. Now she was confused, did she need the wand after all? She turned to pick up the wand but couldn't see it. She turned over onto her stomach to look over the side of the bed. It hadn't fallen on the floor. As she rolled back over, she sat on something hard. Reaching behind, she felt the wand, but when she brought her hand around there was no wand to be seen. The wand was invisible! She could feel it in her hand, solid and heavy but her hand seemed to grasp only air. How had she made the wand invisible?

"I said the magic word to make myself invisible, the same as before," she mused. "What was different this time?" The realisation made her gasp. "I was thinking about the wand! and this morning when I made us all invisible, I was thinking about making a person invisible, not just me." Mollie dropped the wand onto her lap as she suddenly became fully aware of the answer. "It's me!" she squealed in amazement. "The magic is in me!"

Mollie was quite right, the wand wasn't magic, it was just a good quality prop to accompany the magic tricks book that Aunt Hannah had given her. The real magic was in Mollie all along. Mollie concentrated on the wand and said, "Visabilis," and the wand reappeared in her lap. She practiced on the chest of drawers and the picture on the wall, each time displaying a bright unfaded square of floral wallpaper. She concentrated on the plush toy dog among her collection of soft toys and was rewarded with a gap between the teddy and the rainbow horned unicorn. Mollie eventually fell asleep on top of the bed covers.

Later, her mother lifted her into bed and pulled the sheet and coverlet up over her shoulders. As she switched off the light, her mother looked quizzically at the chest of drawers.

I wonder what Mollie has done with the mirror, she thought.

Mollie awoke the next day feeling excited. She was feeling much more confident about doing magic and really wanted to try the spell of flight. The house was quiet, so she tiptoed to her parents' room and peeked in. Her parents were both asleep, her Dad snoring softly, and her Mum curled up in a ball under the covers. She crept through the kitchen and out to the back deck. Max greeted her with a happy yap. She gave him a pat, "You weren't so happy to see me last night, Max," she said. She tipped some dog biscuits into his bowl as a distraction then walked out into the garden.

Mollie was unsure what would happen with the flying spell. Would she grow wings or fly like superman? She said the magic word, "Altivolus." She held her breath as she rose off the ground and her stomach did a little flip flop when she saw the roof of the house below her. She reminded herself to concentrate. When she thought about turning left, she found that she flew to the left and when she thought about turning right, she flew to the right. Mollie practiced flying in a circle around the house and then, feeling braver, she flew over the fence, past the neighbour's house and into the park.

Mollie soared higher enjoying the cool breeze against her face. Flying was fantastic! It was the best feeling in the world. As she swooped downwards, she noticed a man on his early morning run. At the same moment, he looked up and noticed Mollie in her striped pyjamas flying towards him with her red hair flapping in the breeze. He stopped and stared, took off his glasses and rubbed them vigorously on his shirt. Mollie thought quickly. "Inobservatus!" she said hurriedly. The man replaced his glasses and looked around with a puzzled look on his face. He took his water bottle and took a long drink. As he ran off, Mollie heard him mutter something to himself about being dehydrated. Mollie decided that when she was flying from now on it was probably best to be invisible.

Just then, the town hall clock struck eight. Mollie thought that her parents might be waking up soon, so she flew back towards home. She walked into the kitchen as her mother came in tying the sash of her blue dressing gown. She was surprised to see Mollie up early on a Sunday morning and even more surprised that Mollie had already fed Max his breakfast without being reminded. "Why, thank you Mollie," she said. "Now, how about eggs and bacon for our breakfast?"

As Mollie was enjoying her Sunday breakfast, her mother asked her what she had been doing to be up so early.

"Oh, I've just been practicing some magic tricks," she replied truthfully.

"Well, Aunt Hannah will be pleased, she's coming for dinner next week, so you'll be able to show her some of the magic tricks you've learnt."

"Oh," gulped Mollie, "I still need to practice so I'll be good enough."

She had been so busy practicing magic that she'd forgotten that Aunt Hannah had requested a magic show next time she came to visit. She had to learn some tricks to show Aunt Hannah and her parents. She practiced on her friends at school during recess and lunch, and even on Max when he stayed still long enough for her to reach behind his ear to produce a coin. But in-between, she kept practicing her real magic. Her invisible flying was improving, and she had learnt how to walk through a wall.

At the end of Aunt Hannah's visit the following week, Mollie's mother offered her some fresh home-grown vegetables from Dad's vegetable patch. "We have more than we could possibly eat," Mum said to Hannah as she was leaving.

"Oh, thanks Sarah," she turned to Mollie. "Maybe you could carry the bag for me please, Mollie." Mollie carried the bag out to Aunt Hannah's car. "The magic show was impressive," said Aunt Hannah, "although I've always thought 'Abracadabra' was a bit boring." Mollie was going to say, 'me too,' but Aunt Hannah went on, "A clever girl like you would surely be able to come up with something more interesting, like... Aperio."

She took the bag from Mollie who stood on the driveway with her mouth open. Aunt Hannah got into the driver's seat and reached back to put on her seat belt. Then the car door opened itself and from nowhere, a soft warm kiss pressed against her cheek before the door closed again. When she looked out of the window, Mollie was standing on the driveway with a big grin on her face.

"Ha!" laughed Aunt Hannah as she turned the ignition, and before she drove off, she turned and gave Mollie a wink.

About the Author

Margaret lives in a cottage built from mud bricks in a small village in rural New South Wales in Australia.

She lives with her daughter, who is an artist, a dachshund and two cats who visited and decided to stay. Margaret has written a book of poetry, several local histories and collaborated on a children's book with her daughter, about a mythical bunyip.

She works as a Diversional (Recreational) Therapist which is a job she loves and likes to spend her spare time (when not writing) reading, gardening and visiting vintage second-hand stores and markets.

THE MAGIC WITHIN

By Zoey Xolton

Amber sat alone in the far corner of the school yard, shaded by the gnarled boughs of an ancient peppermint tree; it's rough bark home to countless web-weaving spiders, skittering skinks and twitching shield beetles. Legs crossed, lips pursed in concentration, her blunt-cut mousy brown hair falling across her eyes, she lost herself in a story book about distant worlds and marvellous magic. She loved books more than anything. When she grew up, she wanted to tell stories so that other children could find adventure and hope, even when their own lives seemed hard and lonely.

Running her fingers along the pages, she followed the words eagerly. Not even two pages into her new chapter, a shriek nearby pulled her thoughts from the realms of fantasy, and back into the real world. Frowning, she swept her hair out of her eyes and glanced up. The class bullies from two grades above her had cornered a new student, a little girl, against the school fence. They were pulling her long pigtails, laughing, and making fun of her ginger hair and big, round glasses.

Amber felt her stomach twist, and a knot form inside her. It wasn't right. She knew what it was like to be teased and bullied; it was why she sat alone at recess and lunch every day. The same gang of kids taunted her for having freckles and a 'pig nose.' They often called her a nerd or a geek, and would snatch her backpack before dumping it in the boys' bathroom.

No one had ever stood up for her, or defended her. She'd never been good at making friends. The teacher's told her parents that she was socially challenged and preferred her own company to that of others. It wasn't true, of course. Amber had always wanted friends. It just seemed that she hadn't had the good fortune of meeting anyone who really understood her. She didn't want to be just like everyone else; didn't want to change herself to fit in.

Amber liked who she was. If the other children wanted to think that she was weird, or nerdy, and tease her for things like her nose, haircut and her love of books- so be it. She would wear their insults like badges of honour. She liked being a bookworm, and loved how creative she was; and she couldn't very well help how she looked... so who cared what they had to say about her? They couldn't take away her dreams for the future.

Closing her book and slipping it into her backpack, she took a deep breath and strode across the grassy oval, putting herself between the new girl and the bullies. "Leave her alone," she said, holding her chin high, even though she felt anxious and afraid. "She hasn't done anything to you. Why don't you go and pick on someone your own size."

Damien, the self-appointed leader of the bully gang smirked as he towered over her. "What if we don't want to, geek? What are you going to do about it?" he sneered.

Amber narrowed her eyes as she felt a familiar heat rising in her cheeks and an electric tingling dancing over the tips of her fingers. "I might not stand up for myself, but I won't let you hurt her," she said. "Go away, Damien."

"You going to make me, Miss Piggy?" he snorted, pressing on his nose. His little gang of followers burst into riotous laughter. "Go on, you and what army?" Damien's smirk turned suddenly more sinister.

Amber opened her mouth to speak, when she felt small fingers interlock with hers. The new girl with glasses stood beside her, holding her hand. Amber gasped when she felt the tingle in her fingers amplified ten-fold. Energy flowed over and through her. She stared wide eyed at the little girl, who smiled back, giving her hand a knowing squeeze.

"You can't hurt us," she said, speaking for the first time. "My mother says that when two or more are gathered with a common purpose, and share one heart, they will be *heard and answered.*"

Damien moved to seize Amber's collar, his hand stopping short, before recoiling, as if stung.

"Their eyes! Damien! Look at their eyes!" one of his bully cohorts blurted, before they all started backing away.

Amber and her new friend's eyes momentarily glowed an unnatural, intense ice-blue, before fading back to their usual colours.

"Go away," Amber repeated. "Don't bother us again."

Damien shook his head in disbelief. "Freaks!" he yelled, as he turned his back on them, and raced off across the oval to catch up with his friends.

"My name's Amber. What's your name?"

"I'm Jasmine," said the bespectacled girl, adjusting her glasses.

Amber looked down at their still entwined fingers. "Do you want to come and sit with me?" she asked. "I've never met another witch, I mean, outside of my family."

Jasmine beamed. "I would like that," she said. "I've never met another witch either, but I knew we were the same, when you came close, when you stood up for me. *I felt it.*"

Amber smiled back. "Come on then! Do you want to have a look at my Book of Shadows? And maybe, at home time, we can ask your parents if you can come over to play? I got a whole collection of new crystals, and an herbal magic book for my birthday!"

Jasmine sighed and the girls fell in-step with one another as they headed for the ancient peppermint tree. "It's funny how we've always had the magic inside us, but it only shows itself when it's really needed," she said.

"I think that's the secret about real strength, Jasmine. It's the magic that's always inside of us, and we're often stronger than we ever know; just like the heroes from our favourite stories. Having people to care about, having friends worth fighting for, brings out the best in everyone."

About the Author

Zoey Xolton is a published Australian Speculative Fiction author, with a particular penchant for the Dark Fantasy, Paranormal Romance, Sci-Fi and Horror genres. Her works have appeared in several themed anthologies, with many more due for publication, soon! She is also a proud mother of two, and is fortunate enough to be married to her soul mate. Outside of her family, writing remains her greatest passion. She is especially fond of short form fiction, and is working on releasing her own story collections in future; as well as a series of novelettes and novellas. To find out more, please visit: www.zoeyxolton.com!

BIRTHDAY MAGIC

By Sofi Laporte

Kai was cross.

It was his tenth birthday and it seemed the entire world had forgotten about it.

Including his parents!

He scowled the entire way home from school and kicked a pebble on the path. What a miserable birthday it was! No one had congratulated him the entire day. No one had baked him a birthday cake, and worst of all, no one had given him any presents!

His parents were away on a business trip. They had not even called to wish him a happy birthday. Kai was particularly upset about that. He was convinced his parents had forgotten about him.

He was alone with Robin, the babysitter, who skyped with her boyfriend all the time. He was tired of Robin, who treated him like a baby.

"Go brush your teeth," she said, even though he just had. "Put on your pyjamas and go to bed," she said, even though it was only 7pm. The only good thing about Robin was that she'd let him play Minecraft the entire afternoon. His parents never allowed him that. They probably would not like it if they knew that was all he did whenever Robin babysat him. But he did not care.

Serves them right, Kai thought viciously. He would play Minecraft until his eyes fell out. He imagined his parents returning home and finding him sitting in front of the screen with empty holes where his eyes used to be, still playing Minecraft. Kai shuddered.

***

At school, it wasn't any better.

Normally, his teacher, Ms. Snyder, read out all the names of the birthday kids first thing during homeroom, and then they'd sing the birthday song, and then she'd give the birthday kids a small bag with a rainbow coloured pencil, a bookmark and a small piece of chocolate.

But not today, no. Today, Ms. Snyder came in late, breathless and stressed, and she did not read out Kai's name.

Instead, she gave them a spelling quiz.

A spelling quiz on his birthday!

Kai hated spelling. He did terribly on the quiz.

Kai was so cross the entire morning, he did not remind his friends that it was his birthday. They had gone off to play soccer during lunch time and not one of them had asked Kai to come along.

Kai sat alone and poked about his plate of mashed potatoes. He told himself that he did not want to play soccer with anyone, anyway.

When he walked home, it rained.

It was a sad, miserable birthday, indeed.

The entire world has forgotten about me, Kai thought. He had a lump in his throat. Well, fine. If they forgot about him, then he would forget about them, too! He would go live on an island, all alone. Only himself and no one else. And no one would miss him, and he would not miss them. Oh no, he wouldn't!

That's when he kicked that pebble extra hard, and it flew in a nice, high curve right across the wooden fence and landed with a hard thud. Messi would have been proud of that kick.

"Ouch!" a disgruntled voice exclaimed.

Kai stopped.

Now he was in a fine mess! The pebble had hit Mr. Helge's head. He rubbed the back of his head and glared at Kai.

Mr. Helge was a bit odd. He was their neighbour who lived on the first floor right underneath their flat. He had a shock of white hair that stuck out in all directions, and he always muttered to himself.

Mr. Helge didn't like Kai. He always complained to Kai's mother that Kai was too loud, that he should turn down the TV, that he should stop shouting (when the Minecraft game was particularly exciting), and that he should stop playing soccer with his friends in the front yard because they trampled down his newly planted tulips.

And now, Kai had accidentally kicked a pebble against his head and he would surely go and complain to his mother, again, who'd look at him with a sad and disapproving look.

"You know better than that, Kai," she always said.

Kai did know better. Normally, Kai would have apologised.

But on that day, he was so cross with the entire world, that he glared at Mr. Helge.

"I will not apologize!" Kai said darkly. "I did it entirely on purpose! I *meant for* the pebble to hit your head! You can call the police now and have me put in prison! After everything else, it would be the best thing that could happen to me. On my birthday, too!"

There it was. Now he'd only made things worse. Any minute now, Mr. Helge would descend down upon him and drag him to the police station.

Mr. Helge did indeed descend down upon him.

"So, so," he said. "So, so." He towered over Kai and frowned at him with narrowed eyes. They glittered behind those spectacles that always seemed to slide down his thin nose.

Kai found that rather creepy.

"Come with me," Mr. Helge went ahead and opened the door.

Kai swallowed.

Now he was in the suds.

"You should never get into the cars or apartments of strangers," his mother had told him.

Kai felt the crossness well up inside him again. He was going anyway. And if Mr. Helge locked him up and kidnapped him, even better.

Mr. Helge was already inside.

Kai stopped at the threshold, open mouthed.

"Get in and close the door," Mr. Helge said, irritated.

Kai snapped his mouth shut and closed the door. Then he stared in amazement. It seemed like he'd entered a completely different world. Mr. Helge's apartment was not a normal apartment. It looked like the interior of a medieval castle.

"Wow," Kai said. "Cool!"

The walls looked like they were stone. There was a big wooden table in the middle with all sorts of appliances on it. In a cauldron in the corner, something green blubbered. A big, purple wizard's hat and a cape hung on the wall.

Kai had seen these kinds of things only in Disney movies.

"Is this for real?" Kai touched the armour that stood by the door. It seemed real. It also turned its head the moment Kai touched it.

Kai jumped.

"The thing just moved!"

"Kindly do not touch anything and come here." Mr. Helge rummaged in an open chest.

"But Mr. Helge-"

"Where did I put it," Mr. Helge mumbled. He got up and scratched his head. "I must have left it in the cellar." He walked to a door in the back of the room. "I will be back in a few minutes. Kindly sit here by the table and do not touch anything. I repeat: do not, under any circumstances, touch anything." He looked at Kai sternly.

Kai dropped into a chair and nodded. He stared at the appliances on the table. The Bunsen burner was lit, and purple liquid bubbled in a series of vials. *This is cooler than Mrs. Spiller's chemistry lab,* he decided. His fingers itched to touch the little vial that seemed to contain that purple liquid. But then he remembered Mr. Helge.

There was something else on the table, right next to the Bunsen burner. Kai leaned forward to have a closer look at it. It looked like a regular old stick, a bit worn and quite ordinary. It wasn't straight but had bumps. It was unmistakable what it was.

"A magic wand," he said, reverently. He leaned forward and bent over it so closely that his nose almost touched it. "Is this for real?"

He tapped at it with his little finger. Nothing happened. He tapped at it again. Suddenly, a few sparks came out from the tip, like a tiny firework.

"Wow!" Kai was impressed. "This is real!"

Then, throwing Mr. Helge's words into the wind, he picked it up and weighed it in his palm. It felt warm there. One by one, his fingers closed over it.

Kai felt a rush of happiness flow through him.

This felt right.

This felt good!

This was so much better than Minecraft.

He thought a bit. "Accio," he said, remembering his Harry Potter. But it did nothing. "Hm." He tried again. "Abracadabra!"

Nothing.

"Hocuspocus!" he shook the wand a bit.

Not a single spark.

Kai scratched his head. *But before it sparked a bit. Why not now?*

He remembered that he'd been feeling something which he wasn't feeling now: desire. The moment he thought of it, the wand sparked again.

Kai felt excited. The wand turned warm in his hand.

So it was feelings and desire that made the wand work.

Kai thought for a moment about what he desired the most.

He thought about the day today. That it was his birthday. And that no one had even given him so much as a miserable chocolate crumb. He felt sad, and at that same moment, the sparks turned into black smoke.

Kai almost dropped the wand in fright.

"Focus, focus," he murmured. What did he desire?

"Birthday cake!" He imagined it: a three-storied, creamy cake, one layer with white chocolate, the second with strawberry cream and the third topped with the most delicious nougat.

Woosh! And there stood a gigantic birthday cake, exactly as he'd envisioned it.

It was so huge that it pushed the glass bottles off the table and liquid splashed into all directions, spilling into the carpet, burning a hole through it. Kai jumped up and quickly turned off the Bunsen burner before it burned the entire place down. Then he stared at the table in awe.

He'd done magic! He'd just created his own birthday cake! And what a cake it was, too!

He ate until he felt sick from the sugar.

Then he was thirsty.

"Let's see whether this works a second time," he said, and he envisioned himself a huge jar of pink lemonade with ice cubes in it and three straws, a purple, a yellow and a red one.

He'd hardly stopped thinking that when *Whoosh!* There it stood, the jar with pink lemonade.

Kai drank up more than half of the jar and burped.

Magic was awesome! The things he could wizard up! The possibilities were endless! If only he could tell his friends Peter and John and Kurt. How excited they would be for him.

Except, maybe not. They wouldn't be. Not after the way they behaved today.

He could tell his parents. Or maybe not. Not after they'd forgotten about him so entirely.

A dark cloud sank over Kai again. The feeling of certainty that no one really cared for him, that they'd all forgotten his birthday on purpose. And that maybe, just maybe, he'd be better off in this world if he were all alone.

Completely, and utterly alone. Then he could play with this wand to his heart's content!

"Yes, that's what I want," Kai mumbled.

He'd barely finished thinking that, when the wand went *Whoosh!*

Kai looked around uneasily.

Did something really happen just now? Everything was as it was before. The mess of a birthday cake, the half-finished jar of lemonade. The weird medieval room.

Mr. Helge! He should be coming back. What was taking him so long?

Kai went over to the back door and peeked through. There was a spiral stair leading to the cellar. Kai went down, but there was nothing special there. A little cellar room that looked exactly like his mother's broom closet.

And Mr. Helge was not there.

Where had he gone? A feeling of unease filled Kai.

What if his magic had worked, and there really was no one left in the world?

Kai felt queasy. He told himself it was the cake.

He ran up the stairs, taking two at a time, tore the door open and went outside.

It had stopped raining and the birds chirped.

But the odd thing was that there wasn't a single sound. Usually, he'd hear the cars in the busy street, or the airplanes overhead, but it was oddly quiet.

He walked along the street.

There was not a single car moving. Not a single person outside.

"Coincidence," Kai told himself, but now he was getting really worried.

He ran back into the house to the second floor where he lived, right above Mr. Helge's apartment, and rang the bell. But Robin did not open the door.

He took out his key with shaking hands and unlocked the door. Robin was there, wasn't she? He stormed into the kitchen.

But Robin wasn't there. The radio was on, and her cell phone was on the table, and a mug of hot tea. It was as though she'd just stepped out for a moment.

"Robin? Are you in the bathroom?"

He tore the bathroom door open but no one was there.

He took out his cell phone and called his friend, Peter. But no one picked up.

There was no one in the entire flat.

There was no one in the entire street.

There was no one in the entire city.

There was no one in the entire world.

He was all alone.

Just like he'd wanted.

His magic had come true.

Kai stumbled down the stairs to Mr. Helge's flat. If only he could ask him what had happened and how to undo the spell! But Mr. Helge was, of course, gone as well.

Kai nearly burst into tears as the implication of what he'd done hit him, hard.

He picked up the wand and tried to undo the spell.

"I want everything back as it used to be," he said with closed eyes.

Nothing.

"I want the people in this world back! I didn't mean it! It was an accident!"

Nothing.

Kai started to sob.

"You can't undo a spell once you've cast it," said a wizened voice.

Kai jumped and looked around, wildly.

"Who spoke?"

His heart beat hopefully. So he wasn't quite alone!

But there wasn't anyone in the room.

"Hello? Say something else!"

"I said, you can't undo a spell once you've cast it." The voice sounded impatient.

"Where are you? I can't see you."

"Down here."

"Where?" Kai squinted his eyes. He looked under the table, down on the floor, behind him.

"In the corner to your left."

Indeed, someone sat there.

In front of a tiny hole, sat a little grey mouse.

"No, impossible! Did you speak with me?"

"Nothing is impossible, and yes I am speaking with you."

"But how?"

"When those vials crashed on the floor, a dollop of magic potion dropped on my head. This gave me the ability to speak."

Kai's head whirled. "You said I can't undo this spell."

"Nope. That much I know, from having watched the grand sorcerer at his magic day in and day out."

"The grand sorcerer? You mean Mr. Helge?"

"Pah. He is Merlin himself."

Kai looked at the mouse in disbelief. "Mr. Helge! Merlin!"

Then he remembered that he's made him disappear, too. "Everyone's gone because I, uh, wished them gone. I never thought it would actually happen. How can I undo it?"

"You can't. Magic that is cast, is cast."

Kai paled. Was he going to have to live alone in the world forever and ever?

"But you can use another kind of magic to rewind time."

Relief flooded through Kai. "That's it! How do I do it?"

"See that cuckoo clock on the wall? It's magical. All you have to do is rewind it to the time you want it to be. I've seen Merlin do that several times."

Kai went to the cuckoo clock and thought. It'd been 3 pm when he left school. It took him 20 minutes to walk home. That's when he must have met Mr. Helge. So he'd be safe enough if he rewound the clock to 3:10.

"How do I do it?"

"Simply turn the minute hand."

"Thank you," Kai said.

"No problem. And if you ever happen to have a piece of cheese for me, you know I would appreciate it."

"Definitely."

He wound the hand of the minute back to 3:10.

Something rushed in the air.

Colours zoomed by. Kai felt dizzy.

All of a sudden, he stood again on the road, halfway back home.

The noise of the traffic surrounded him. There were people on the sidewalk, bumping into him. He nearly ran into a man with a briefcase.

"Watch out where you're going," he grumbled.

Kai nearly sobbed with relief. He was so happy, he skipped all the way home.

Oddly enough, though, Mr. Helge was not working in the front yard.

Kai raced up the stairs to his apartment.

When Robin opened the door, he almost hugged her.

"I am so glad to see you!" he burst out.

She looked at him in surprise. "Well you're in a good mood. I guess it's because it's your birthday. Happy Birthday, Kai. There's a surprise waiting for you in the kitchen."

Kai went to the kitchen. A big birthday cake stood on the table. Chocolate and strawberry. Very similar to the one he'd wizarded up himself.

"Happy Birthday, sweetheart," a voice said behind him.

"Mom! Dad!" Kai threw himself at them.

"Our plane was delayed and we could not contact you. Did you think we'd forgotten all about you?"

He buried himself in his mother's arms and nodded. "Kind of."

"You know we'd never forget about you, ever." His dad ruffled his hair.

"I know that now," Kai said.

"Your friends also called and asked why you didn't play with them at lunch time and why you ran away so quickly after school." His mother placed both hands on Kai's shoulders. "I told them to come over for a little party."

Kai blinked rapidly to get rid of that suspicious burning feeling in his eyes. He wasn't crying. No, he wasn't!

"That's awesome," he managed to say, and blinked a little harder.

The doorbell rang.

"There they are already," his mom said and started to arrange colourful paper plates on the table.

Robin went to open the door and returned immediately.

"There's an old man out there wanting to see Kai." She shook her head. "He looks a bit like Gandalf in jeans."

Mr. Helge stood by the door with a slim box. "I heard it is your birthday today and I wanted to give this to you. It is time for you to have it."

Kai looked at the thin box and knew what was inside.

"It's a wand, isn't it?" He crossed his arms behind his back.

"One of the most precious wands ever made. It is yours. As a birthday gift."

Kai took a big breath. "That is very kind of you, but... no thank you."

Mr. Helge nodded slowly. Something twinkled in his eyes. "Another time, then." He emphasised the word, *time*.

"Another time," echoed Kai.

Mr. Helge winked at him and left.

"Who was that?" asked his father as he helped himself to a large piece of strawberry-nougat cake.

"Oh, it was just – Merlin. He wanted to give me a wand," said Kai. "But I said no thanks. I couldn't handle all that magic, you know."

"Very funny," Robin said with a full mouth.

Kai laughed.

What a nice birthday it turned out to be after all.

About the Author

Sofi Laporte was born in Austria, grew up in Korea, studied Comparative Literature in the U.S.A., and lived in Ecuador with her Ecuadorian husband. She enjoys writing fantasy and paranormal stories for children and Young Adults. When not writing, she likes to scramble about the beautiful Austrian country side exploring medieval castle ruins. She currently lives with her husband, 3 trilingual children, and a cat in Upper Austria.

TOADSTONE

By Vonnie Winslow Crist

It all began with a toad—an especially fat, olive-green toad who hopped out from under a boxwood bush right in front of Jared Jones. Luckily, he reacted quickly enough not to step on the creature.

"What are you doing here?" asked Jared as he knelt down.

The toad blinked its golden eyes several times, but said nothing.

"You don't belong in the middle of the sidewalk." The boy picked up the amphibian and carried it to the edge of the green-space which stretched between the long rows of townhouses. "I think you will do better in the woods."

The toad looked at him, then grasped his right forefinger with one of its front feet. The amphibian's hand-like foot felt cool and dry against Jared's skin.

"How about here?" he asked the toad as he sat on the ground not far from Thorny Branch, a small stream which wound its way through the green-space. Thorny Branch eventually emptied into Velvet Rock Lake. The lake, edged by mossy rocks, began beyond the turnaround at the end of the road where Jared lived in a three-story townhouse with his mom and dad.

"You will be safer in the woods away from skateboards, bikes, and cats," he explained. "Besides, there are lots of bugs to eat and clean water to drink." He patted the toad's bumpy head and added, "I bet the soil near the stream is soft enough for you to dig a hole in. Then, you can hibernate here from autumn until next spring."

Jared lowered his hands to the grass and opened his fingers.

The toad did not hop away. Instead, the amphibian turned around, stared at Jared, and opened and closed its mouth several times—almost as if it were speaking.

Leaning closer to the toad, Jared whispered, "Are you trying to tell me something, fellow?"

After nodding its warty head, the toad jumped from his hand onto the ground. Then, the creature turned around to look Jared square in the eyes. After it raised one of its front feet in a gesture which seemed to say, *wait*, the toad crept beneath some raspberry bushes at the foot of a maple tree.

Feeling a little foolish for waiting, Jared pulled a paperback book out of his jacket pocket and started to leaf through the pages. After locating the torn piece of paper he had used to mark a page last night, he scanned the paragraphs to find the exact place where he'd stopped reading.

"There it is," said Jared as he tapped the page with his finger. "Now, let's see what happens to the dragon next."

Before he could finish reading the page, Jared felt a sudden weight plop onto his lap.

It was the toad. Appearing to smile, the green-brown creature sat on his blue jeans holding a clear pebble in its mouth.

"What do you have there?" said Jared as he put down his book and reached for the toad.

In answer, the creature leaned forward and spit the now slimy pebble into his hand.

"Gross!"

Even though he wanted to toss away the slippery stone, Jared forced himself to study the thing. It almost looked like a piece of quartz that you might buy in the rocks and gems section of a craft store—but there was something weird about the pebble. It was cold. Not just a little cold—but ice cube, glacier cold. Plus, it had a slightly blue tint to it.

"What is this?" he asked the toad—expecting no reply.

"Toadstone," answered the amphibian before it hopped back into the shadow of the sticker bushes and maple.

Once in a shaded spot, the toad transformed into a foot-high, man-like being dressed in a blue pull-over shirt, tan pants, dark brown boots made of fur, and a pointed red cap.

The little man doffed his hat, bowed slightly, and said, "I am Brickleburr Wartley, at your service."

"Brickleburr Wartley!" exclaimed Jared. "What sort of name is that?"

"A respectable gnome name," said the little man. "A name you should remember, since I was sent to give you the toadstone."

Jared looked at the quartz pebble which he held in his hand. "What is so special about the stone?"

"It is magical," replied Brickleburr. "I would have thought a boy who reads about dragons, wizards, and Greek mythology would know a magical thing when it is given to him."

"You must have me mixed up with someone else," said Jared as he shook his head. "No one in my family has anything magical about them. We are just everyday people. Mom is a secretary at my school, and my dad works as a mechanic at the We-Fixit Garage on Main Street."

"Oh, I have the right boy," replied Brickleburr. He popped his hat back on his balding head. "Magic in the blood is not necessary. A person needs only to see the magic in the world around them." He placed his arms on his round belly, then continued, "After dark on clear nights, you go to your window, wish on stars, and spot the trolls behind the trash dumpster."

"They are probably just shadows," said Jared with a sigh.

The gnome smiled, then continued, "When you sit in your yard on sunny days and squint, you recognize that some of the butterflies flitting about the flowers are really fairies."

"It is just my imagination," Jared argued as he plucked a dandelion from the weeds beside him, closed his eyes, made a quick wish, then blew the fuzzy seeds into the air.

The gnome laughed, then said, "What about the dragons you watch in the woods? Others only see gnarled tree branches, but you know that dragons watch over the children playing in this park."

"It is no more than an optical illusion—a trick played by shadows and light on my eyes," replied Jared as he tossed the toadstone from hand to hand.

"You sound like your parents," said Brickleburr. "But a boy who whistles songs to the birds, drops crumbs on the ground for pixies, ties bits of yarn on the honeysuckle vines in the green-way for elves, and helps wayward toads stay safe—believes in magic."

Jared picked up the toadstone and held it pinched between his right forefinger and thumb. "Let's say I think you are telling the truth, what do I do with a toadstone?" he asked.

The gnome smiled. After stroking his beard several times, he explained, "After I shift back to toad-shape, pick me up, press me gently against your chest with your left hand, walk toward Thorny Branch, and while holding the toadstone in your right hand—think of a door, tap the pebble on the side of the biggest hickory tree you find, then, open the door and step inside."

Still doubting what he had seen and heard, not to mention the word of a gnome, once Brickleburr Wartley was back in toad-form, Jared did as instructed. When he had nearly reached the bank of Thorny Branch, he stopped in front of an enormous hickory. Feeling rather foolish, he tapped on the side of the tree.

There was no missing the smile on Toad Brickleburr's face when a door opened in the huge trunk. "Step inside, Jared," said the disguised gnome, "for a world of magic awaits you."

Realizing he had just used magic to open the hidden door, Jared grinned, stepped into the tree, and gasped as a world beyond his imaginings shimmered before him.

About the Author

Vonnie Winslow Crist is author of the young-adult-friendly *The Enchanted Dagger, Owl Light, The Greener Forest,* and other award-winning books. Her magical stories are included in *Curse of the Gods, Dragon's Lure, Hoofbeats: Flying with Magical Horses, Ocean Stories, The Great Tome of Fantastic and Wondrous Places,* "Cast of Wonders," "Amazing Stories," and elsewhere. A cloverhand who has found so many four-leafed clovers she keeps them in jars, Vonnie strives to celebrate the power of myth. For more info: http://www.vonniewinslowcrist.com.

THE FEATHERED CLOAK

By Edward Ahern

The trouble began when Rhys found the oak wardrobe. He stood barely four feet tall, but the free-standing closet was twice that high. Its hinges were beaten brass, turned brown with age. The carved wood was riddled with little worm holes. Rhys had never seen a piece of furniture so big and heavy, and he knew that if it fell on him, he'd be squashed.

The wardrobe rested in a corner of a large, open attic. The attic was a jumbled clutter of his grandfather's collection of magic equipment. His grandfather had been a professional magician who had starred in New York and Paris and even Moscow.

The key to the armoire doors stuck out of the lock. It turned with a dry rasp. When Rhys opened the doors, piles of theater costumes, tablecloths and curtains spilled out onto the floor. Their colors, once shocking bright purples and pinks, had faded over time into pastels.

I'm in trouble, Rhys thought. He pulled out the rest of the clothes so he could restack them and shut the doors. Under the cloth, worms had eaten through one of the base boards. Beneath the rotted board, he could see the shape of a box.

Rhys touched the riddled board, and it broke into dusty fragments. *I'm* so *in trouble*, Rhys thought, as he reached in and pulled out a yard-long wooden box. The wood was different than the wardrobe, darker and denser. Peculiar symbols were carved all over it, and on the top was written:

'Numquam Mutare Pallium In Flavo'

The box was untouched by worms. Rhys looked back into the false bottom of the wardrobe. *Odd,* he thought. *There's no latch or hinges. This was sealed into the wardrobe. I don't think my grandfather ever knew it was here.*

Rhys reached down and pulled off the lid. He stared again, this time at gray-brown feathers woven together. The feathers were big, bigger than seagull wing feathers, bigger even than turkey tail feathers. And when he touched the feathers, they sparked into sharp oranges and purples.

Rhys dropped the feathers in shock, then bent back down and picked them out of the box. They were a coat, no, not a coat, a cloak. As he held it, Rhys watched the feathers pulling back into themselves, shrinking until they were a size that could wrap around him.

The cloak continued to sparkle where he held it. *I wonder,* he thought, and swirled the cloak around himself. He was covered chin to toes. The cloak was comfortingly warm, like a snow suit on a cold winter day.

It burst into shiny black, then red, then purple. *I wonder,* Rhys thought, *maybe green?* The cloak shifted into greens. First the color of a fall granny apple, then the shade of deep winter ocean, then the dark green of spring leaves, and lastly the green of a summer frog. And Rhys could feel the skins of apple and frog against his skin, the wet of sea water and the damp of new leaves.

He tried to do other things, but the cloak didn't make him strong, or let him fly, or give him a chocolate cake. Still, the colors were brilliant, and swelled Rhys' feelings, making everything more intense.

He took off the cloak, put it back into the box, and paused. *I can't tell mom or dad. I'm only nine, and they'll take this away from me. I'll put it back where it was and only take it out here in the attic.*

The next day after school, he clambered back up the narrow stairs into the attic. When he took out the box, he almost dropped it. There were new words carved on the box, and one of them looked like his name.

Rhys, Caveat flavi.

Rhys had no idea what the words meant, and took out the cloak. It was still his size, and sparkled again when he touched it. He turned the cloak sunset red and felt the dwindling warmth of day's end. He changed it to the dark blue of his eyes and suddenly he could see past his school to the highway. And then, as he thought of the highway, he was hovering over it, staring down at passing cars from what seemed to be the height of his attic.

Rhys panicked, and was immediately back in the attic, the cloak again a dull gray brown. *I can go places, kind of. Or at least I can see them.*

That was blue. What else? Mustard yellow, he thought. But nothing happened. *The yellow of fire!* Still nothing. Rhys became angry.

I order you, he commanded, *to change into the yellow of gold.* It was perhaps his order, or perhaps his anger, but the cloak shifted into the buttery glint of gold. Rhys felt the slick coldness of the metal, so pure that he knew if he could bite it his teeth would leave marks.

But something was different. Rhys felt as if the gold color reached far beyond the cloak, as if he had just let something loose that was rampaging further out than he could see. He took off the cloak and put it away.

That evening, his father paced back and forth excitedly. "What a day I've had, Rhys. The stock market is up three percent and my own investments are up five percent. We're a lot richer today than we were yesterday."

Rhys' father kept talking with his mother about buying things, about taking vacations, about schools for Rhys. But his father didn't sound happy. He just talked about getting more things.

When Rhys put on the cloak the next afternoon, he wasn't his usual cheerful self. *Give me the dirty yellow of a dying fire,* he ordered. As he stood basking in cooling embers and ringed by ashes, he felt the sadness of presences ending. *This is so uncomfortable it's painful,* he thought, put the cloak away and went downstairs.

Rhys' mother and father called him into their bedroom the next morning.

"Rhys," his mother said, "your great aunt Clarice died late yesterday afternoon. She had been sick for a long time, so I guess it was her time, but she's gone."

"And lots of other old people," his dad whispered to his mother. "It's as if someone had encouraged them to finish their lives. Very strange."

That day at school, Rhys said almost nothing. He felt like he'd gotten lost in the woods, or had done something really bad that no one knew about. As he walked from the bus stop back to his home, he noticed a woman standing on the sidewalk in front of his house. She was very old but somehow still beautiful, strawberry colored hair half covered with a babushka, clothed neck to wrist and ankles in soft beige and green. Rhys blinked and she was standing next to him.

"Rhys, stop. You and I must speak."

Her voice had the gentle echoes of wind.

"I'm not supposed to talk to strangers."

"I was called Jörd. You're tied more closely to me than you know, and know me much less than you should."

"But you're still a stranger."

"What sign would you need? Ah. Look closely at this picket on your wooden fence. Do you know what tree wood it is under the white paint?"

"No."

"It's a spruce that grew in Canada." Jörd touched the wooden slat. "Look at it now."

As Rhys stared at the picket, it sprouted, with no noise or fuss, a green needled sprig.

"Wow," Rhys exclaimed. He still hesitated, but Jörd radiated the comforting ease of his grandmother's hugs. "Okay, I'll listen."

"You've found the cloak- don't bother to deny it! The cloak has adopted you, even though you're dangerously ignorant of its powers and perils. Why didn't you obey the warnings?

Rhys was puzzled. "Warnings? Oh, you mean the symbols on the box. I don't understand them."

Jörd sighed. "Time turns wisdom into error. When the words were carved, Latin was the common language of the world, known to millions of people. Now it's dead to all but a few scholars. The writing told you never to turn the cloak yellow.

"You can transform the cloak into any color you wish, and learn how each color heals, how the colors blend, and how you can reach outside yourself. But never again change the cloak into yellow- flavum. The shades of that color are used only for evil."

"But what if I think of a yellow color? I can't stop thinking. And why is yellow evil?"

"You can think all you like without harm, just never command the cloak into yellow-not straw, not pus, not gold, not sand, not amber. Yellow has wonderful shades, little one, and once was as the other colors. But it was used for horrible purposes, and those who do horrible things have used it since."

The old woman was frightening Rhys. "Could we just burn the cloak?"

"My Rhys, the cloak feathers were taken from the ashes of a bird that never dies. They can't be destroyed by fire. And you're its guardian now. Deep down you already know that you want to keep it."

Jörd touched two fingers to Rhys' forehead. They felt mountain firm. She kept them pressed against his head while she talked.

"Your actions have awakened another who will come to take the cloak from you. He must not get it. He'll lie and try and cheat you out of the cloak, and if that doesn't work will try to kill you. Never, ever, agree to his entering your house. Here is knowledge of the cloak which I hope protects you."

Images poured like a waterfall over Jörd's two fingers into Rhys' head. He saw the strength of green, the unmagical stability of brown, the mingling and stripping of a thousand colors. Rhys staggered when Jörd broke the contact.

"I must be elsewhere and everywhere, Rhys, and can't stay. You must behave like your namesake."

"Huh?"

Jörd sighed again. "The things parents don't tell you can hurt you. Both you and your name are Welsh. Rhys means ardor and enthusiasm. It's the opposite of what the other stands for. That's your birthright. Use it to counter the evil coming at you."

Jörd walked away without another word. Rhys felt like he was lost and scared in a dark chamber, but finally decided that what Jörd had told him must guide him onward. For several afternoons, Rhys went through rainbows of colors, exploring what he could see and do. He discovered that if he wished for no color at all the cloak became invisible, and Rhys just looked like he was wearing his ordinary clothes.

On the fifth day, a man came to Rhys' school.

His jacket was the color of bug guts, the yellow of a rotten peach. He talked with Rhys' teacher, Mrs. Burton, who asked Rhys to come out of the class with her.

"Rhys," she nodded, "this is Mr. Flaves."

When the man smiled, Rhys could see yellowed teeth.

"Mr. Flaves has apparently lost something, and thinks that you know where it is."

Rhys felt himself trembling, but his voice stayed firm. "Mrs. Burton, I don't know Mr. Flaves. What's he lost?"

"What have you lost Mr. Flaves, and where?" From her tone, Rhys knew that Mrs. Burton didn't much like Mr. Flaves.

"Ah, I'd rather not say, but it's precious to me and I think that Rhys knows where it is, don't you boy?"

"No, sir, I do not. And I don't know you. Can I go back in now, Mrs. Burton?"

"Yes, Rhys, you may. Mr. Flaves, this all seems very irregular. Unless you have something more specific, I'm afraid you'll have to leave the school."

The man looked at Rhys like he wanted to rip out his throat, but smiled enough to show his yellow teeth again. "I'll keep looking, won't I, Rhys?"

When Rhys came home from school that afternoon, Mr. Flaves was sitting in the living room with Rhys' mother and father.

But I didn't invite him in! Rhys thought

"Rhys, this is Mr. Flaves. He seems to think that you found something of his."

His mother and father looked strained, as if they regretted letting Mr. Flaves in. But Mr. Flaves had the look of a dog about to tear apart meat.

"Thank you, Mrs. Cardiff, for letting me in. Rhys, would you invite me in as well?"

"No! Never! Get out of our house!"

"Rhys," his father barked, "manners please. Apologize to Mr. Flaves."

"Never! By that which I have worn, I order you to leave! Never enter again."

Flaves jumped up from the sofa and began cursing. At least it sounded like cursing, Rhys didn't understand the words.

As he hissed at Rhys, yellow spittle sprayed from his mouth. "Little toad, I will be upon you when you least expect it." And he backed from the house, glaring at Rhys and hissing curses.

Rhys' mother and father called the police, and everyone questioned him about Mr. Flaves. But he just kept repeating that, no, he didn't know Mr. Flaves, and, no, he didn't have anything that Mr. Flaves owned. *I'm not really lying,* he thought, *I don't know Mr. Flaves and I do know that he has no claim to the cloak.*

The police drove by Rhys' house several times a day, but after two weeks, his parents and the police forgot about the episode. Not Rhys. He knew that Mr. Flaves was waiting for his chance to pounce.

Jörd's lore surged like tide inside him. *It's pushing at me to be understood and used,* Rhys thought. Every afternoon, he scooped mind water from Jord's knowledge and practiced a new skill with the cloak. *Flaves is ready to hurt me just as soon as I'm alone. I only have one chance to protect both me and the cloak.*

On the day when there was no more of Jörd's knowledge to absorb, Rhys got off his bus one stop early, waved goodbye to his friends and started walking alone toward home. Flaves was on him before the first minute had ticked by.

Flaves was dressed in his long coat the color of rotten peaches. "You can't run from me, you little brat."

"I'm not going to."

"First, I'm going to reach in and rip apart your puny little mind. I'll order you to bring me the cloak. After that I'm going to use this," Flaves pulled out a bronze dagger, "and slice you open from navel to neck."

Rhys had never been so scared, but he knew what he had to do. "There's no need to send me for the cloak, I have it on." And Rhys changed the color of the cloak he was wearing from invisible nothing to purple, dark brooding royal purple.

Flaves stumbled back a step, but then jumped forward again. "All the quicker to cut you open."

"Flaves, go away now without the cloak. You'll be disappointed, but still be who you are. If you attack me, you'll be changed into something you hate, and still won't have the cloak. Please. Go away."

Flaves' coat swirled with ugly yellows, the colors of old bruises and pond scum and dead fish bellies. Gnarled yellow fingers sprouted from the coat and grabbed at Rhys.

As Rhys jumped back, he flung jagged spouts of purple at Flaves, spouts that twisted and squeezed the yellow fingers. Flaves screamed in pain. The purple pounded like waves over him, frothing and hiding Flaves from view. When it ebbed away, the man who stood there was dressed in dull brown. "What have you done to me?" he wailed. "What am I?"

"You're an empty husk now, Mr. Flaves. Yellow and purple are contrary colors. When I merged them, they created a special brown. Drab, powerless brown. You're of no harm to anyone but yourself now. Walk away."

Rhys never saw Mr. Flaves again. A year passed, during which Rhys became adept at using the cloak, being careful to never order it into yellow. But over time, he began to feel that playing with the cloak for his enjoyment was almost insulting to it.

One day, using the blue of his eyes, he was skimming at tree top through a forest of oaks and maples. Far below, in a clearing next to a huge oak, he saw an old woman with red hair, dressed in green and dark brown. Just as Rhys recognized her, she looked up and smiled.

My little Rhys, she thought. *I've waited for you to come. You protected the cloak well.*

Jörd, thank you for your great help. I wouldn't be alive without you, and the cloak would have been lost. But why am I now feeling uncomfortable in it?

Sweet child, it's time for you to grow up, at least a little. The cloak is not a toy, and you are not its owner, just its steward. You will do wonderful and magnificent things with the cloak, but for others and not for yourself. Now fly off and enjoy my forest, feather steward, for I must be elsewhere and everywhere. But know that I wish you well.

.

About the Author

Ed Ahern resumed writing after forty odd years in foreign intelligence and international sales. He's had over two hundred fifty stories and poems published so far, and five books. Ed works the other side of writing at Bewildering Stories, where he sits on the review board and manages a posse of four review editors.
https://twitter.com/bottomstripper
https://www.facebook.com/EdAhern73/?ref=bookmarks

THE MARVELOUS SWEET SHOP WITH NO NAME

By Rima El-Boustani

Magic is uninteresting, normal. Wizards are witches and witches are wizards. Everything is backwards in this land of make believe. The flowers are green and the grass is purple. The wizards wear brightly colored dresses and the witches dress in trousers and shirts. The sky is brown and the Earth is blue.

Everything behaved in a way it shouldn't. If something should be bright it was dark. If it should be heavy it was light. Everything was so unpredictable it could easily be predicted and so wonderful that everyone was bored.

In this backwards land, there existed a sweetshop. But this shop did not choose to follow the rules. Its sweets were weird and wonderful, as sweets should be. They were made using magic. They were not bland or boring as the sweets should be in a land where everything is in reverse. They were magnificent, resplendent, superb – words could not describe them.

James watched children go in and out of the sweet shop every day. He longed for a sweet – any of them would do. Children emerged from the shop, clutching bags of sweets bought by their parents. But James was poor. He could not ask his parents for money to use on sweets. Instead he sucked his tongue, while imagining what the fluorescent chewing gum that never lost its flavor or the candy canes that could turn you into Where's Waldo might taste like.

One day, James sat perched on a floating wall by the roadside just outside the entrance to the sweet shop, which, incidentally, had no name. He waited for the proprietor to open the shop and tried to look normal and inconspicuous. But as usually happens when you want something too much, the opposite happened. And so, while James tried to blend in the background, his hair turned a brilliant pink and his skin glowed emerald. It would be impossible for a blind person not to have noticed him. The owner, whose name was Imper, and had the use of both his eyes, certainly did notice the poor little boy.

He called James over, beckoning him to enter the shop, which smelt of everything at once. James breathed in heavily, his nostrils filled with all the fabulous smells from the sweets inside. James had never felt so good.

As James approached nervously, Imper said, I have need of a boy for a job. Would you like a job that will pay you with all the sweets you can eat? Wonderful sweets, too.

"Yes," James replied, ever more eager.

"Good. Come inside then, the walls have ears. I don't want my rivals to hear." Imper confided as James entered the shop. "Well then, the job I have for you is simple. I need someone to make these sweets magic. It is a tiresome job. You have to do each sweet one by one or the magic doesn't work."

"Why won't the magic work?" James asked, almost regretting his job.

"That is the curse of this wonderful land. If I had made the sweets boring, it would be done in bulk. You see sweet shops on all the street corners; shops that don't smell of flowers in bloom, that don't give children green ears for a day when they chew on a gum drop, that won't make your hair fall off in patches and patterns. If I had sold ordinary sweets, it would be nothing. I could easily make and sell those in bulk. But I wanted to sell these marvelous creations. These things no one has heard of. The problem is, because everything is backwards, sweets, which ideally should be fantastic, must be boring. So, I have to jinx each one by one."

Imper's speech over, James accepted the job though it seemed an impossible task.

He set to work first on Gobstoppers. He had to turn ordinary Gobstoppers into magnificent balls that would bounce first in your mouth and then in your tummy. They were supposed to do this for a week. Then there were the blocks of bubblegum that blew too many bubbles while you chewed them. There were beans that would grow edible trees if you planted them. These could feed a family for a year.

The work was hard and tiresome, but as this land worked backwards, such hard and tiresome labor must necessarily be easy and fun. James came every day to his job and left every day with an armful of sweets to take home. The irony was, because this made him happy, he could only feel sad. And so ends the tale of poor James Smith, who had an ordinary name but was not ordinary himself and who lived an unordinary life filled with fabulous magic and wonderful sweets more magnificent than anyone could imagine.

About the Author

Rima is a prolific writer who loves all genres. She studied Development Studies and Human Resources as well as an art year. She is fluent in English and Swedish. Rima was published by Words and Brushes for their Ekphrastic challenge.

THE BEGINNING OF A LEGEND

By Bella Guerra

"You're late!", Master Beron growled at Peter, who entered the busy inn with drenched clothes, sneezing. "What took you so bloody long? You were supposed to water the horses! For six blimey long hours I was being told off by four customers that their horses are dehydrating! Four customers!"

"I'm sorry, sir! I swear it was not my intention." Peter looked at him anxiously.

"Yeah, right, for keeping your head right up in the clouds!"

"But, sir, the handle broke off and the bucket tipped so I-"

"Don't throw your pathetic excuses at me! You should be glad that Jedys and I took you in from the dying Humean land, and I expect straight obedient, respectful and hard-working servants at my inn in return! You know I have a family to take care of! One more step off the line, boy, and I'll see to it that you and your brat sister are thrown out on the streets! Now, get out of my sight!"

With one smack to his head, Peter raced to the kitchen, not noticing more water being spilled by his fast movements. As soon as he had settled the bucket at the table, he let loose a deep breath. Master Beron was in a good mood, indeed. That was the second time this year Peter had survived the half-goblin's rage with no black eye or a limping leg. The Gods had answered his prayers!

Sighing, he shook his sore hands from carrying the heavy bucket and made his way to the stables. Five horses, four of them mute, were standing patiently in their stalls with nothing to drink for the past few hours. Peter hoped that the water left over in the bucket would quench the horses' thirsts. One by one, he filled the smaller buckets beside the horses with fresh water and his own bucket became lighter and lighter. Once he reached the last horse, there wasn't a single drop left. Distraught, he let his bucket drop and could only shake his head to the horse, who tilted its head in curiosity and observed the tired boy.

"Well, human?", the last horse spoke to him in a gentle voice.

"Can't you see? There's no water left for you." Peter drew in a shaky breath, "I'm sorry! I was clumsy and lazy when I fetched the water!"

Surprisingly, the horse only looked at him with that same curious manner. "What are you talking about, human?", it tilted its head further to the side.

Before Peter could reply to it in frustration, the horse continued speaking, "Why did you say there is no water in your bucket when it is clearly still full to the top?"

Confused, Peter looked down to his bucket to see in shock and amazement that it was filled to the brim, nearly overflowing the old bucket. Dumbstruck, he finished filling the last bucket while wondering to himself how in the heavens the bucket could have refilled itself. Had he had hallucinated the light weight of the bucket due to lack of sleep?

"Not bad for, what do they say, ah yes, a *Humean scum,*" the horse commented smugly. As Peter was about to retort back, the talking horse fell into a deep slumber, its loud snores filling the whole stable. Peter hated the term so much because it spoke true to who he really was.

Humean scum.

Humean. Old Fanseyan for human servant. A human was worth nothing in Anderling because they had no magic.

***

The following day was greeted with beautiful weather full of sunshine and also with strong wind. A beautiful day for Hallows Eve in the Northern border. A day when every citizen entered into a state of disarray, a future wytch or wizard, ranging from five to thirteen years of age, would be chosen from each kingdom. Families of fairies, fauns, centaurs, minotaurs, elves, wood nymphs, goblins, leprechauns, and all those mixed with other races, gathered themselves in the town-center to celebrate.

Benches and tables were set up, along with tents full of beverages and delicious meals (a proven comfort for those devastated parents whose children were not chosen as a wytch or wizard.) Entertainment such as clowns walking on stilts, fire breathers smoking out shapes of animals, acrobats balancing on high tightropes and a marching band playing the national anthem of the Northern Kingdom, paraded through the whole town. Children followed the parade train with delight while guessing what kind of magical trait they would have if chosen. With them were the two children from the self-indulgent inn keeper, Beron and Jedys. Both wore proudly their bright blue Sunday clothes and were covered from head to toe with all sorts of gold rings, necklaces and bracelets.

In the meantime, the poor orphan Peter, together with his eight-year old sister, Leannah, had stayed behind to keep the household clean for the half-goblin family they were made to work for, to continue celebrating in the house. All the guests joined the innkeepers to celebrate the festival. Everyone except for humans. After all, why would they join in the festivities if they weren't even qualified for being chosen as wytch or wizard?

Leannah changed the bed sheets and dusted all the walls and ornaments, while Peter washed the windows and mopped all the floors. As Leannah was carrying a basket full of wet sheets to the laundry line, she spotted a lone old man walking on the road passing the inn. He shielded his face with his patched straw hat from the blowing wind and his whole body leaned against his walking stick as tiredness took him over. From his patched, grey clothes and battered leather sandals, one could easily recognize him as a Humean beggar. Such beggars tended to search for bonded labour: to work for a master in exchange for food and shelter.

Without hesitation, Leannah dropped the basket and ran towards the old man, who was about to collapse from exhaustion.

"Sir, let me help you." ,Her little voice piped up as she gently grabbed the old man's arm and guided him to the entrance. The old man rambled out some words of thanks and appreciation as Peter stepped out of the doorway.

"Lea, why isn't the laundry hanging? I don't want us to get in-"

"Pete, he's tired! He needs some rest, otherwise he will fall flat on the floor!" his sister cried in response while lowering the tired pilgrim onto the staircase. "Please Pete, help him!" ,Her shiny, childish eyes pleaded at him.

At first, Peter swore at the Gods and at Leannah's selflessness, but eventually, he gave in.

"All right, I'll bring him water. But you must know Master Beron will be furious when he learns about this. He thinks Humeans stain everything they touch."

Peter returned with a mug of fresh water just as a loud howl and a gigantic wave of wind passed over the town. The howling wind knocked away the old man's straw hat, and after a fascinating ride with loops and sways, the worn-out hat was caught by the branches of a towering redwood tree.

Right then and there, the wind stopped.

All three stood there and stared at the hat several feet above them before small Leannah dashed towards the tree.

"Oh, little miss, you really don't have to retrieve that old thing. I can make myself another one," the raspy, calm voice of the old man protested while he watched the skinny girl climb herself up the tree towards the outstretched branches holding the hat. By the time he spoke, however, she was already higher than the inn itself.

"Lea, please, come down! You're going to hurt yourself!" Peter shouted with worry.

For a while, it seemed like Leannah could control the situation as she effortlessly managed to reach high enough to grab the straw hat with her fingertips. Then her foot stepped on a faulty branch and it snapped in two. A long scream escaped her throat as she tumbled down the ranging redwood tree.

Peter's heart felt as if it stopped dead in his chest. A panic swelled through him, making his hands shake and his fingers tingle. A strong force of some kind seemed to flow through his arms, like something yearning to be free of its imprisonment. For a long moment, Peter battled against this unnatural source, but by and by, he gave up and let the source go. It left him dizzy and devoid of energy, so it took him a moment to grasp what he was seeing.

His sister was *floating* midair as if something invisible had caught her from the deadly impact with the road.

He noticed the old man looking at him strangely, and that's when Peter realized his own arms were outstretched, aimed towards his sister. He lowered them slowly, and as he did, Leannah sank down to the ground at the same pace. *This could not be happening!*

Peter saved Leannah with magic!

***

It was agreed that the Humean beggar could reside at the inn until the owners returned from the festival later that day. The siblings quietly resumed their household work while the old man observed them both, asking them personal questions from time to time.

"Our parents died from a revolt against wytches," replied Leannah to the man's question about their childhood.

"We were found on the streets," Peter added. The man turned his questioning to what Peter had done to save his sister from falling from the tree. "Has something like this happened before?" the old man asked softly.

Peter's face turned scarlet red and he tried to hide it by scrubbing a clean table. But there was no use hiding his secret.

"It was in the stables," he mumbled. "For one moment, the bucket was empty and I still had to provide the last horse with water. Then in a snap, the bucket was filled up to the brim again and I--"

The conversation was abruptly interrupted with the innkeeper's family entering the near-empty building. All their laughter and chatter stopped at the sight of the old, ragged man.

"Good evening, dear misters and mistresses," the old man greeted kindly and tipped his retrieved straw hat in respect.

"What is a Humean scumbag like you doing in my household," Jedys, a full-blooded nymph, snarled at him and bared her sharp teeth.

"Oh, I was on a journey to the capital but when I reached this town, my knees gave away from too much walking. Fortunately, these two children have kindly given me hospitality and time to recover. I still feel a bit shaky from the long walk, so I hope that I can stay one hour longer to recover more." The old man favored them all a smile.

In one sudden movement, the whole family snapped their heads towards the orphaned siblings. With a brave heart, Peter pulled his sister behind him to prevent any harm from coming her way.

"Jedys, take our children upstairs," Master Beron told his wife with a controlled voice while staring at the siblings with fiery eyes.

As soon as the mother and children were out of the room, chaos erupted.

"Haven't you put yourself already into enough trouble, boy?" the horned creature shouted at Peter.

"Calm down, sir!" The old man interjected, "There is no need to make such a fuss over a little thing-"

"Over a *little* thing?" Master Beron spat in a dangerous tone. "I want this house cleaned from all the dirt that has entered inside. Dirt such as this *humean* scum! I want to have everything perfect when the Protector arrives-"

"The Protector is already here, Beron!", new voice boomed, coming from none other than the old man. With a snap of his fingers, his appearance rapidly changed into that of a young, handsome man. The Great Warlock Erathon.

Dressed as a warrior with a mail shirt hidden behind a leather surcoat, the well-known Warlock Erathon wore his signature mage cloak with hood and an elegant staff. In an instant, Beron fell to his knees and bent his head to avoid the warlock's sharp stare. Peter and Leannah gaped at him in shock, then scrambled onto their own knees.

"Please, stand up. I hate it when you do that," Erathon chuckled, his eyes twinkling at the orphans. The children slowly rose to their feet, amazed. "Master...Master Warlock," Beron gasped flabbergasted, trying to catch his breath. "Why, it...it's such an honour...for you to re-reside in...in our household-"

"Silence!" Like thunder, the warlock's voice rumbled across the room. Then with a calm procedure, he approached the children.

"The tradition on Hallows Eve speaks of the Protectors of the Nine Kingdoms selecting a child with a future gift of magic which will be exposed on that same day. No matter from what race, species, or status, this child will be given an opportunity to achieve things no normal wytch or wizard on the common ground could ever achieve. Beron, you know of these rules, correct?"

The eyes of the innkeeper widened as he pondered the question and nearly sky-rocketed through the roof with delight.

"Of course, your highness... I mean... Erathon, the most powerful, the most wise. I will call my children down immediately!"

"No," Erathon spoke softly and placed a hand on Peter which sent a striking wave through the boy's body, giving him more confidence. Peter stood up straight and proudly. "Earlier this afternoon, I witnessed this young man, or as you may call him, your *servant*, manipulating the winds to stop his sister from falling off a tree. My hat flew away and the young lady kindly volunteered to fetch it back for me. That is when the incident happened. You know the rules, Beron. I need to take the boy with me to the Mage Council along with the other eight children, to be sorted as an apprentice under the given wytch or wizard with similar magic traits."

The smile on Beron's face disappeared as quickly as it had appeared.

"But…but…it's *impossible*. There has never been an incident, where a *humean*, a weak species, was found wielding magic! It…it seems like a myth that something like this could happe…"

"Yes, of course! And now it's happened!" The warlock turned to face Peter. To speak the truth, it will not be easy living a life as a mage apprentice. You will face many dangers and your own fears. There will also be rivals, or even enemies of whom you will have to fight against. Furthermore, you must prove yourself and put hard work into your talent. Especially as you come from what some may regard as a 'weak' species. However, I would be honoured if you'd accept this offer and I would see to it that I apprentice you myself. You hold great power, Peter. There hasn't been a girl or boy I've seen as strong as you."

"I protest!" the confounded innkeeper chimed in. "I swear to you, warlock! He will never leave my custody and he will never leave this house, because he is my property! Along with his brat sister! None of them will leave this house!"

"The longer he stays, the more dire the situation becomes! For now, Peter must be trained in order to control his powers. Throughout time, with his magic oppressed it could lead to dangerous outbreaks that could severely harm those around him... and even bring death." Erathon explained in a frustrated manner.

Beron was about to retort an insult back at the warlock, when a third voice entered the conversation.

"I will." Peter took in one big breath before he repeated his answer again, louder. "Yes, I will! I want to come with you!"

Groaning out loud, Beron grabbed his horns as he pondered the warlock's remarks. Now Peter knew why the innkeeper was so hesitant to let him go when he despised the boy so much. Letting Peter go meant one servant left in the household. Peter simmered with anger at the thought.

In the fullness of time, Beron's tense shoulders sagged down as if he'd defeated in a heated debate. "Fine," the half-goblin grumbled. "Take the boy. Take him far away from here."

A small sob escaped from Leannah's as it came to her realization that she might never see her older brother again. With misty eyes, Peter squeezed her hand in sad farewell. But to great luck, the warlock noticed the sorrowful exchange between the two siblings.

"One more thing, Beron! I would like to take the girl with me as well-"

"Take them both! Just make sure I never see them again for the rest of my life."

To that. the siblings joyfully hugged each other.

What a day it had been! First, they discovered Peter had magical powers. Now, they were set free under their forced livelihood in the inn. It was a beginning of a legend.

***

With a final blow, Zetharim, the White Sorcerer, beheaded the last Necromancer of Darkness with his sword, Lightbringer. Black clouds separated and the first summer light shone through. Panting heavily, the White Sorcerer looked up to see the soldiers of the Royal Elven army cheering him and King Leor.

He did it. He saved the world.

Looking around, he spotted Queen Leannah running towards them. She kissed her husband, then hugged her brother.

"You did it, Peter. Now you truly are the Protector of the Nine Kingdoms."

And for the first time since the start of the war, Peter smiled.

About the Author

Bella Guerra is a high-school student, history maniac, movie geek and book nerd. Whenever she is not attending classes at an Austrian international school, you can find her in a small house in the countryside, lost in the world of fantasy and literature.

COOKIES AND MILK

By Eddie D. Moore

"Eat your green beans, Abbie."

"I don't like green beans, and you can't make me eat them."

Abbie's mother folded her arms and tapped a finger against her elbow. "If you don't clean your plate, you can't have a cookie. All four year olds have to eat their vegetables."

"I don't care." Abbie turned her head and stared out the window to avoid her mother's glare.

"Okay, fine. You can march your tail upstairs to your room and don't come out until bedtime."

Abbie grabbed her mermaid doll from the chair next to her, gritted her teeth and walked out of the kitchen in three quick steps. As she climbed the stairs, she stomped on each step until she reached the top. She wanted to slam her door, but she knew just how far she could push her mother and that a slammed door would bring her pounding up the stairs. She closed it with a gentle click and then threw herself onto her bed.

After bouncing three times, Abbie placed her mermaid at the edge of the bed and said, "I still want a cookie."

Abbie stood up on her bed and then jumped into the air. She landed on her bottom with a satisfying bounce. Her doll was tossed up and over the side of the bed. She threw out an arm in a futile attempt at catching her mermaid, knowing that she was too far away.

She blinked when her hand closed around the doll and stared at it unbelievingly for several long seconds. Did the doll jump off the floor to come back to her? If so, she didn't see it. She reached for it and it simply appeared in her hand.

Abbie dropped the doll at her feet, stared at her red shoe in the corner and reached for it. The shoe appeared in her hand, and she giggled to herself. She dropped the shoe and then reached for her stuffed unicorn. She dropped the unicorn and reached for her pink pony.

After dropping the pony, Abbie closed her eyes, pictured her mother's cookie jar in her mind and reached for a cookie. She opened her eyes and saw that she held one of her mother's chocolate chip cookies. It was still slightly warm from the oven and smelled wonderful.

She took a bite and jumped off her bed and said to herself, "All I need now is a glass of milk."

A minute later, she was pouring a glass full of milk. She sat the milk jug on her nightstand, and helped herself to another cookie. She dipped her cookies in the milk and lost count of how many she ate.

She reached for another cookie but nothing happened.Closing her eyes tight, she tried again, nothing. She smiled when she remembered the ice cream in the freezer and was soon eating spoonful after spoonful.

The bedroom door opened and Abbie dropped what was left of the ice cream. Her mother looked slowly around the room. Her eyes stopped on the cookie crumbs on the bed, the milk spilt on the nightstand and the box of chocolate ice cream that was beginning to melt.

"Your father and I have wondered when your powers would manifest." Her mother sighed, shook her head and smiled. "I want you to know that I'm not mad at you, but I want you to promise me that you won't summon anymore treats for yourself from the kitchen."

Abbie sniffled and nodded her head. She forced herself not to grin when she remembered that the supermarket has a whole isle of snacks and goodies.

About the Author

Eddie D. Moore travels extensively for work, and he spends much of that time listening to audio books. The rest of the time is spent dreaming of stories to write and he spends the weekends writing them. His stories have been published by Jouth Webzine, Kzine, Alien Dimensions, Theme of Absence, Devolution Z, and Fantasia Divinity Magazine. Find more on his blog: https://eddiedmoore.wordpress.com/.

NO FIREBALLS AT THE KIDS' TABLE

By Rennie St. James

"It'll be okay."

Austin hid his face from his sister but kept his voice strong. "I'm eight, not a baby. I know it'll be okay."

Ava patted his shoulder even as her sigh was dramatic enough to ruffle his hair. "I'll see you inside."

He waited for his twin to leave before he stood. She knew him too well - he would be terrified if he was a baby. The magical lessons that had been told to him repeated in his head, but they were jumbled. Was he supposed to breathe in or out when he lifted his arm? Look east... or was it west? He did know his fast heartbeat wasn't good. Magians had to be the calm in the center of the storm. It was the only way to handle the magical energy they could move and use.

Tapping his hand against his leg, he paced around the small room. It wasn't one he'd been in before, but there were always whispers on the playground. Secret ceremonies. Shared wisdom. Power. Magians were taught magic from birth, but they couldn't use it until the Knot approved them. The Knot was what non-magical people called a coven, just as they would have called him a witch, wizard, or warlock. Austin was a Magian though. He lifted his head and puffed out his chest.

"I am a Magian. I am a Magian."

It was helpful and annoying that his twin had already been through the ceremony. Ava was brainy enough for the both of them. Her report cards always glowed with a rainbow of flying colors. His grades were darker colors and a few even hovered off the page. Their parents said it didn't matter as long as he did his best, but Austin had never been entirely sure.

Whenever their teachers spoke of magical energy, they used the example of a ball rolling down a hill. The bigger the ball, the harder it was to stop. Emotions stirred up energy; physical size could store energy. Adults had both. There were rules governing Magians, but any adult had enough energy to roll right over him. They made the decisions including when it was time for each kid's ceremony.

They said he'd understand 'when he was older', but Austin was the oldest he'd ever been and he still didn't understand.

Running a hand over his head, he scrubbed at the slight pricks of his hair returning. It didn't calm him. His ears felt hot so he scratched at them next. More magical lessons floated in his mind.

'Be calm and steady.'

'Energy is everywhere - we all have magic inside us.'

'Power lies in control, not in chaos.'

A deep breath did help calm him. Austin nodded as the words became clearer in his mind. He wasn't a straight-A student like Ava, but he had studied his entire life. The Magian history and prominent families were things he could repeat whenever a teacher asked. Science classes included regular non-magical lessons but also spells using the four elements. Math wasn't just about trains traveling at the same time; their homework included herbal calculations for potions.

"I am a Magian." Repeating the words aloud did make Austin feel better. His parents were members of the Knot and they believed he was ready. He had to be ready.

"Austin." A robed man stood just inside the open door. "It is time."

He nodded but kept his head high. The man's longer legs meant Austin had to shuffle quickly to stay by his side. Looking forward, he ignored the gathered crowds of other Magians. He couldn't ignore the heavy heat of the air – he almost choked on it. It wasn't just a crowded room, the adults had been using magic. Energy still buzzed and hovered in the air. More lessons flashed in his mind.

'Energy isn't created - it is moved. Sometimes, it is stolen.'
'Loss balances out the universe.'

That wasn't his favorite lesson, but everyone said it was important to understand. Austin shuddered at the painful memories. Colorful sparks brightened the room, and he turned eagerly to the distraction. Ava winked at him; his parents smiled and nodded. Austin knew his energy would mix with theirs and the others - for better or worse. He wanted it to be for the better.

A large round table was centered in the room. It was where the adults sat for Knot celebrations and there were always celebrations.

Thanksgiving. Winter Solstice. Christmas. New Years. Life was about celebrating blessings and his Knot did that often. Kids, like him, were kept at the kids' table though – protected, but away from the fun. This ceremony was him moving up to the adults' table.

He almost plowed into a small table before realizing the man leading him had stopped. Austin reached out a hand to steady himself then stared at the large vase on the table. The dark blue color didn't interest him – it was the numerous cracks lining it that drew his gaze. It was as if someone had broken it then tried to put it back together. He almost snorted at their efforts. Ava had broken their mother's favorite vase and he had fixed it without either parent realizing it.

Several members of the Knot stepped forward to form a circle around him. Others circled the large dining table, and still others were spread throughout the room. When Austin turned, he saw his sister and parents once more. Ava again sent another shower of colorful sparks from her fingertips as she grinned at him.

"Austin, it is time to use your magic for the benefit of others. Call on the energy inside you and bring fire."

He recognized the elderly man but still stared at him. When the man frowned and gestured, Austin turned back to the vase. Did they want him to burn it? It wasn't the best repair job but that seemed like a harsh response.

"Light the fire above the chalice. Control and hold it there." It was a woman who spoke and she smiled kindly at him. Mrs. Flint had been his second-grade teacher.

There were no magical lessons or advice in Austin's head now. He stared at the vase – frozen like a kid caught with his hand in the cookie jar. Energy burned his back. Without turning, he grinned at Ava's prompting. She hadn't told him what would happen, but she had his back. Literally.

Closing his eyes, he felt the energy still swirling in the room. He imagined colors for each person's unique spark and could see the rainbow. Breathing out, he turned to the right and lifted his hand. Austin opened his eyes in time to see the sparks shoot from his fingertips.

The flames sputtered out instead of forming a fireball. He wanted to run from the room without ever looking back. Maybe he could join the circus or—

Hands landed with warm thuds on his shoulders and he had to abandon the thought of escape. Austin darted a look up at the guards who would imprison him for his failure. His mother met his gaze with a smile. She squeezed his shoulder and heat flowed from her touch. Austin felt the same reassurance on his other side and looked up to his father. A small energy ball again zapped his back. Ava.

His family still loved him.

"Again, Austin." The elderly man didn't glare when he gave the command.

Energy and color swirled inside the room and inside him. The sparks from his hand grew into flames – orange and red dancing flames. Other colors joined them, and Austin turned to see everyone with one hand lifted. Together, they were strong.

Blues mixed with the oranges and reds then greens and pinks joined them. The flames curled inward and grew into a brilliantly colored ball.

"Hold it still." Again, Mrs. Flint encouraged him.

Austin didn't need to look around to know the others had lowered their arms. He held the storm of magic together – hot, almost painfully so, but it was his. His first attempt at magic, well, his second really. He'd done it. He stared at the fireball then noticed the jagged cracks in the vase were glowing.

"It is time to light the fires. Everyone together."

He could feel each person take a spark from his fireball. Candles he hadn't noticed before came to life at once. The entire room was filled with a happy, golden glow. His magic hadn't been dimmed by sharing it. The colorful fireball pulsed with energy and life.

"Austin, lower the fireball into the vase."

It was the first time he noticed his arm trembled. Austin's breath was also coming in harsh pants as he slowly lowered his arm.

The fireball sank into the vase with a hiss. As he watched, a new jagged crack glowed brightly.

Applause and cheering almost made Austin flinch. His response was hidden from view as his parents and sister hugged him. It was Ava who leaned in close so that only he could hear.

"Isn't this great?"

Austin accepted his parents' kisses but stayed close to his sister's side. He turned to her with a grin. "Oh yeah, they don't allow fireballs at the kids' table!"

About the Author

Rennie St. James shares several similarities with her fictional characters (heroes and villains alike) including a love of chocolate, horror movies, martial arts, history, yoga, and travel. She doesn't have a pet mountain lion but is proudly owned by three rescue kitties. They live in relative harmony in beautiful southwestern Virginia. The first books of Rennie's fantasy series, The Rahki Chronicles, are available now; however, a new series is already in the works for 2021.

MISS PHILLIPS

By Christine King

If you find this after I am gone, then you will know the truth.

I think my teacher is an alien.

I know that sounds crazy, but nothing else makes sense.

Miss Phillips has huge bug eyes, magnified by her giant glasses, her hair is always pulled back into an iron like bun. Even her long fingers, thin and claw like, creep me out.

She speaks with a grumble and sometimes when she shouts, little bits of spittle fly from her mouth. Her teeth are yellow, and her skin is pale white. Maybe she's a vampire? Maybe a zombie? But I think she is an alien from outer space, sent here to torture little kids with heaps of homework and impossible sums.

She never lets us speak. I think she must need us silent so she can hear the transmissions from her home planet, instructions on how to defeat the children of Earth and make them her silent, compliant, slaves.

Right now, I am hiding in my room. You see, I have no one to tell about this terrifying discovery.

Tell my mum? Too late.

You see, I think my mum is in on it.

Hard to believe and yet…

Yesterday was the parent-teacher meeting. I was sitting in one of our blue classroom chairs, swinging my legs and listening to my mother speak to my alien teacher. I was waiting, hoping that my teacher might give herself away. I wanted her to say something that might make my mother realise she was speaking to an alien.

Then without warning, in the middle of a chat about my behaviour and how Miss Phillips had seen me goofing off instead of working, (which wasn't strictly true, I had been drawing pictures of spacecraft ideas, ones that might have brought Miss Phillips to Earth) my mother said quite seriously.

"Miss Phillips, I am impressed, you have eyes in the back of your head."

I almost fell off my chair.

I didn't even know about that, no wonder she can see everything that I do.

Humans don't have eyes back there, so my mother must know that Miss Phillips is an alien, and she isn't even bothered by it.

Conclusion: my mother is in on it.

Help! What do I do now?

I am hidden in my room but tomorrow I have to go back to that mind draining classroom and face my teacher.

Of course, you haven't heard the worst of it. I thought to myself that I would need to find out once and for all if Miss Phillips is indeed an alien, and if she is, I needed proof. How else can I tell the authorities about my alien teacher?

My mother, the conspirator, stood outside the classroom talking to another mum, and I asked if I could play a game on her phone. She handed it over and continued her chat.

I took the phone and put it into video mode.

Miss Phillips was in the classroom, her back to the door, sorting paperwork, awaiting the next parent.

Carefully I opened the door, silently I sneaked past the tiny chairs, up to my teacher. My heart beat fast, my hands shaking as I reached out. In a swift movement, I pulled at the iron hard bun, and yanked it aside, hoping to reveal her extra eyes.

She spun around snarling, ruining my shot and my view of the back of her head.

Her cries brought in my mother, who apologised to Miss Phillips (while my teacher tucked her hair back into the bun) and hauled me out, yelling at me.

"What on Earth were you doing?"

I stayed silent and let her drag me to the car.

In the back seat I sat, my mother still raging.

I watched the footage on the phone and there, just for a moment, I saw them, eyes, hidden under the hair, watching, shocked and angry.

But now I have to go back to school. Who do I tell? My mother obviously knows and couldn't care less. Now, Miss Phillips knows that I am on to her.

If I disappear, then someone, please, look at the footage and come find me.

I may have been taken to another planet.

A silent, compliant slave forced to do impossible sums and never-ending homework.

Save me!

About the Author

Christine King is a female horror writer, she has a book of short stories available on line and has been fortunate enough to have some stories and poems included in anthologies and magazines.

She will soon have published a series of six children's fantasy books.

Visit her author page here:

http://christinekingauthor.wixsite.com/mysite

She enjoys a good cocktail and loves archery, she also runs a group on Facebook to help female writers get into the male orientated genres.

Christine is a wife, mother and Child minder. Her influences are Stephen King, Mary Shelley and her young daughter.

QUEEN ZOE AND THE SPINNING GAME

By Randee Dawn

As far as Queen Zoë was concerned, the new year – which was less than 24 hours old – was a bust.

Outfitted in her heaviest, clompiest hiking boots, she hurled herself into the inn's great front room and scouted for something to knock over. She spied a plastic toy crèche set up on a nearby table, kicked a wooden leg and sent Jesus, Joseph and two wise men flying. A little rock fence flopped over after a will-it-won't-it moment of wobbling. Mary remained kneeling, like she was praying not to get kicked.

That made Zoë feel better.

For a moment.

Then the noise of Kevin's birthday party started up again. Voices of the adults rose and fell like waves, plates and glasses clattered up a storm. She swore she could hear the sound of cake being cut, and eaten. But what cut through it all was her little brother's burbling, a sound he made whenever he was tired. Or happy. Or basically feeling any emotion at all. Right now, she could tell from the way the burble sounded that he was bored.

Bored! Who could be bored at their own birthday party?

That was Kevin, though, top to tail. He'd been like this for the last five years, when he'd been born right in the middle of Zoë's perfect only-child life. He'd arrived red and squalling and sickly, six weeks early – and he'd totally ruined Christmas. Both of her parents cared about nothing for the rest of the year, until he came home from the hospital.

Clearly, her parents wanted a boy all along. A quick look at the huge crate of presents he'd received earlier that night revealed how much more everybody loved him than her. Kevin got boxes of Lego sets, a Hot Wheels track, and an air hockey game. Meanwhile, everyone still thought Zoë was interested in princesses and fairy wings. She might call herself Queen, but that was *not* what she wanted under the holiday tree.

But Aunt Maeve was different. Only her mother's adopted sister was even the slightest bit creative when it came to presents. She sent books and magazines and how-to-build things kits – everything just a year or two ahead of Zoë's interests – and by the time she got around to reading them or playing with them, her thanks were so out of date it was embarrassing to say "thanks," so she just never said anything.

Kevin's presents were the ones Zoë preferred. She'd watch him as he tore through the wrapping paper and tossed aside gift after gift, as if the whole reason for presents was to unwrap them. He never acted like he cared what he got, or how much he got, or whether he'd even use it or not. He usually spent the rest of the evening ripping the paper up into smaller pieces.

Kevin got everything. He could do anything. He wouldn't even have to go to school like Zoë. They said he had "special needs." Never, to Zoë's mind, had a bright line been drawn more clearly between the first-born girl and the precious, important last-born boy. She knew the score.

And if she could have, Queen Zoë would have taken her royal indignation, envy and – though she'd never admit it – weary sadness out the door and down the highway, never to be seen again. But tonight, it was 26 degrees out; the ground was hard as bone and the air as piercing as a scream. Besides, her coat was upstairs on their guest room bed, smothered under a large pile.

The front room would have to do. So that's where she was, right now. Wanting cake, but not wanting to go back and ask for it.

She guessed it wasn't a bad place to be exiled to. The inn's Christmas tree still sparkled warmly in one corner, twinkling lights reflecting off of red braided hazelwood balls and handmade figures of owls, raccoons, deer, and sparrows. They were deep in the mountains of Pennsylvania and everything around here seemed to be about nature or cabins or skiing or sometimes all three at once. The rest of the lobby area was taken up by the inn's check-in desk, a winding staircase and three rocking chairs made from curled tree branches.

As for the floor, well, it was covered with the wrecked remains of baby Jesus' birth.

The light was low and cozy while a gas jet-fueled fake fire crackled in the fireplace, while overhead, songs by ancient singers the Beatles drifted down from the speakers. Zoë felt soothed by the music, right up until the moment she remembered she was supposed to be furious. She was in a state of high dudgeon – a word she had read once and remembered because it reminded her of *being* in a dungeon. Which wasn't so far off from reality.

Zoë spotted a single upholstered, striped chair; a cushiony pillowed seat set off-center from the rest of the room, a piece that did not belong amongst the rest of the décor. She leaped into it, swallowed into the throne of her choosing, small hands braced on the chair's arms and chin pointed firmly into her chest. This was the perfect position to pout, so that's what she did, jutting her bottom lip forward and clinging to the anger inside of her. Chunks of short dark hair grazed her cheeks and covered her chocolate-colored eyes. Her toes just touched the floor, so she bent them this way and that, arcing first to the right, then the left.

She guessed she had maybe three minutes until someone – Kevin, probably – came to find her. There was no rest from big sisterhood; what was so funny about everything was that Kevin really, really loved her. He'd practically worshipped her ever since he could focus his eyes long enough to see his big sister. Over the years, he'd often gotten in trouble for doing many of the things Zoë had talked him into, and never put the blame on her. He would follow any order she gave him, except for the only one she cared about: *Go away*.

Zoë's toes slid across the inn's creaking wooden floor, the rubber soles of her boots dragging as the circle widened. Despite her attempts to hold on to her irritation, the music, the lights, and the solitude were working their way into her heart and calming her down. She understood this was how life was: Kevin was the special one in the family. She was just the rough draft. Six years from now, she could escape into college and never look back. Until then, she just had to get used to it.

Out of the corner of her eye, the ceiling jiggled.

Zoë paused, squinting upward. Blinked hard once. Twice. Then directly above her head the painted crossbeams of the ceiling clearly rippled, the way the lake out back would from a stone skipped over it. The rubbery circles widened, then contracted again, as if something had passed through and briefly disturbed the structure.

Zoë waited for another ripple – but it didn't come.

She began swaying in her chair again. Soon she'd have enough momentum to spin fully around. To complete a circle, to spin and watch the world revolve around her would be so satisfying. She could be at the middle of things again. Finally, Zoë felt ready for the big push. She kicked off with one leg and started flying, her sour expression morphing into something like joy.

She stopped hard, the force jerking her out of the chair. She stumbled onto the floor and froze in place.

Something was in the room with her. It crouched on the winding staircase in the corner, sharp taloned fingers clasping the spindles, a shadowy face obscured by the winding evergreen garland. Zoë was about to make a screeching, terrified cry when the creature leapt directly into the air and landed on the banister with the grace of a bird.

Zoë's tongue dried up.

The creature was easier to make out now by the light of the holiday bulbs. It was a person or a kind of person no bigger than Zoë herself, with a large head and small hands that ended in those long, weirdly-pointed fingers. Messy strands of white-blond hair sparkled when it cocked its head to one side, revealing a pale, gleaming face. Wide, tapered eyes flashed dark green at Zoë, evaluating and absorbing and finally knowing everything about her in the space of a single breath.

"Pray continue," said the being, in a voice that danced and tickled Zoë's ears. "Ye was doin' fine, my Queen."

"What was I doing?" the gaze held her in place, like a caress on the top of her head.

"Seemed to me like ye was startin' the spinnin' game," it said. "An' doin' a mighty fine job of it, too."

She nearly objected to having it called a game, but Zoë liked the idea of getting credit for doing something right. "What's the ... spinning game?"

It laughed and she thought she heard bells. Then it was as if the creature both slid and melted to the floor at once and in a blink – it was standing before her, hands clasped behind its back. The cloth it wore, a belted robe of sorts with a hood that dangled far past its waist, flowed around it like a mist, shifting colors every minute or so.

"I know it all," said the creature. Up close, she gave off a scent reminiscent of Zoë's backyard garden – dirt, curled roots, bruised fruit – and seemed like both boy and girl. Zoë decided she was a girl, and the moment she mentally made that leap, those extraordinary features shifted the way the creature's clothing did – and she had high cheekbones and long eyelashes. Zoë knew she'd made the right choice.

"'Tis an easy one to learn," she said. "All's y'do is spin and spin until it happens. Get someone to help, that's the usual way, an' if yer anchor spot is true, all 'tis needed is a bit o'wantin'," she said.

"Wanting what?"

"Wantin' from yerself and wantin' from the other side." She glanced up at the ceiling, precisely where the ripple had come from moments earlier. "There's somethin' ye want, isn't there?"

Of course Zoë wanted. She wanted so much; she was nearly thirteen and the world was full of things she could not have.

"O'course y'do," said the being. "Like heat, comes offa you." With that, she plucked Zoë's headband off of her scalp with a touch that yanked several hairs out with it. Zoë yelped, but got no apology from the creature, who tossed the headband into the seat of the chair, then took a step backwards.

"Bring the seat thisaway," she gestured, and Zoë grabbed the chair's arms, sliding it to the right an inch, then two.

"'Tis truly placed now," said the creature. "Now, start afresh."

Zoë made to climb into the seat again, reassuming her throne, but the creature made a throaty growl. "Thass a bold move, Queen Zoë," she said. "Y'don't take the seat unless y'mind bein' what's wanted, y'understand?"

Zoë backed off and frowned, face pinching in thought. The creature watched her with curiosity, but no impatience. And then – she thought she had it. Clutching the back of the chair, Zoë began running clockwise, her big boots once again clomping against the wooden floorboards. She ran faster, then faster, not just the center of the universe this time but the one actually making it turn – and when she finally released the chair, she stumbled back, dizzy.

The chair spun and spun like Zoë's head, and she could hardly stand to watch it. She felt a little sick to her stomach.

There was a soft "pack" sound – not quite a pop, not quite a click; it came with a bit of hardness at the end. The chair slowed, and then stopped. The headband was gone.

Zoë gaped, woozily whipping her head around to see where it must have slid off to, but it was not on the floor and not anywhere in sight.

"There now," said the creature, whose hair seemed less awry and full of glitter.

"Where is it?" asked Zoë in a thin, tight voice.

The creature wriggled her pointed fingers and raised them into the air. "Where'd y'suppose, child? To them that wants."

"What if I want it back?" She wasn't sure she did; only that she did not like the idea of having done something irreversible. Impossible and irreversible.

"Y'can't," said the creature. "'Tis someone else's prize, now."

"Whose?"

The creature winked at her and touched the side of her tiny nose. "'Tis not your'n to know. But 'tis appreciated, so it is. Ye can be certain o' that."

"Is it gone forever?"

Again came that bell-like tinkle of delight. "Forever. Ever and forever. 'Tis a longer time, my Queenie, than neither ye nor I know of." She slid her green gaze back to the chair, which Zoë now beheld with a measure of awe. "O'course, tha's tiara 'tis but a trifle, yes? There are … other things y'be wantin'?"

Zoë took a step back, her heart going *thumpa thumpa* in her ears. She closed her eyes, overwhelmed, and let the quiet settle in. She wondered at the way things that seemed permanent and impossible might actually have some bend in them. Like crossbeams in an old inn's ceiling.

Burble burble burble.

Queen Zoë flashed her eyes open and turned to the noise. Kevin stood just inside the French doors separating the dining room from the foyer, making his wet mouth sounds. He had a flat, empty look on his face that changed the minute he spotted Zoë, and then he became the brightest spot in the room.

"It's my birthday!" he crowed. "I'm five!"

Without even turning back, Zoë knew the creature was gone – if she'd ever existed. She reached up to the crown of her head, but her hair was loose around her ears. The headband was really gone. She felt wild, uncontrolled. A growling noise in her head began like static on the radio, and she let it grow.

"Play with me!" said Kevin, who never asked, only demanded.

"How … about … a new game?" Zoë asked. Her voice sounded far away, not her own. When he nodded enthusiastically, dropping a toy on the ground, she pointed. "Get in the chair."

He clambered up, needing a little boost from Zoë to make it on his own. She positioned him like a doll against the cushions, the noise in her head filling up every little extra space, drowning out reason. She began swaying the chair this way and that, from left to right and then clockwise.

"Wait!" shouted Kevin, looking up at her. "I feel all funny."

"Is it like a tickle?" she asked.

He shook his head, reddish-brown curls bouncing. "Spin me?"

"That was the plan."

"Will I fall out?"

Zoë scanned the room, snatching up the fallen faux-rock wall from the tumbled crèche and laid it across his stomach. "There. That's your seatbelt. Now you can't fall out."

Kevin beamed and put the palms of his cool hands on her cheeks. She flushed beneath his touch; Kevin was not a hands-on child, and sometimes screamed if you surprised him with a hug or a kiss. He was an alien, she reminded herself. But then she also realized this might be the first time he'd purposefully touched her. "Safe," he said. "Safe with my seed-belt."

Zoë set her hands on the back of the chair. Slowly, she began turning, the static growl in her head turning up again. Her boots clomped like elephants on the floorboards, and somewhere, she heard Kevin whooping with delight. "Love this!" he cried out.

Harder, faster. She was sure it had not been so difficult to turn the first time.

"I am not going to sleep!" he shouted, a sentence that made no sense to her.

"Then just dream," she called back to him. "Close your eyes and dream."

"I'm not dreaming!" he refused, yet his voice sounded fainter. Zoë mashed her eyes together, dipping her head down with the strain of pushing. "This boy doesn't like dreaming!"

And then – a "pack" sound. Not a pop, not a swoosh. Just like before.

Zoë released the chair and collapsed. Above her, she felt a light breeze as the bottom of the chair flew by her once, twice, three times … and slowed down.

Silence.

After a long moment, Zoë opened her eyes and sat up on the floor. The chair had come to a stop in front of her, its seat gaping like a mouth. It was empty. Empty, except for the fake rock seatbelt.

"Thank'ee," came a lilting, musical voice. "Oh, thank'ee very much, Queen Zoë."

But there was no one in the room.

Light-headed, Zoë nearly threw up on the old wooden floor all of the cake and ice cream she'd had earlier that evening. She got up on her knees and reached into the seat of the chair, then buried her face in the cushion, taking deep breaths. It smelled like a well-tilled garden in there.

She was an only child again. She had done it, too: This was all on her. She knew about the spinning game, she'd put Kevin into it, and won by losing him. No one would ever know it had been her, not if she kept her mouth shut. It was everything she'd wanted for the last five years.

She thought about how he'd put his hands on her cheeks. "Safe," he'd said.

And that brief happiness turned dark and cold, creeping up from her gut into her head as she slowly comprehended the terrible thing she had just done. It had been completely unworthy behavior from a girl who thought she deserved to be called Queen. Who believed totally that she was a good person, at least right up until these last few minutes.

It wasn't so much that she missed Kevin.

But she needed him back.

If she was going to call herself Queen, she'd better live up to the title.

Zoë moved so fast she could barely think. She yanked a red hazel ball from the tree – one of Aunt Maeve's books had said that hazel was an object of power, and it seemed like something she should have with her right now. In any case, it was the best she could do on short notice. She also grabbed the plastic wall – Kevin's "seatbelt," the last real thing he'd held in this world. Then she threw herself in the chair, again swallowed by its back cushions. Secure in her seat, she dragged her toes on the floor, turning this way, that way, harder and harder, spinning, spinning.

A high wail of challenge grew in her throat and she let it out, thrusting one hand in the air. Wanted or not, she was coming. She would take back what was hers. Zoë lifted her feet off the ground and went around, around, around, her face wide with joy and determination.

There was a soft "pack" sound, and the chair spun on its own, holding to its true place.

Queen Zoë was on her way.

About the Author

Randee Dawn is an entertainment journalist by day, fiction writer by night based in Brooklyn. Her fiction has been published in magazines and anthologies including "Fantasia Divinity," "Where We May Wag" and "Children of a Different Sky," and she is the co-author of "The Law & Order: SVU Unofficial Companion." You can find all kinds of other magical things about her at randeedawn.com.

UNICORN SATURDAY

By Carol Ann Martin

Even before he found the unicorn, Gus somehow knew that this wasn't going to be an ordinary day. There was a tingle in the air with a feeling that something mysterious was about to happen.

It was a wintry Saturday and Gus was helping Uncle Jack set up his market stall. He unwrapped a newspaper bundle and there it was — the beautiful china unicorn. It was blue with a silver mane, tail and a silver horn. It stood as if prancing like it was about to leap away somewhere exciting.

Just holding it in his hands made the magical tingle feel even stronger. Together, Gus and the unicorn could have had all kinds of adventures. But Gus had no money to buy it, so he put it back on the market stall.

Uncle Jack sold bric-a-brac. There were teapots, jampots and honeypots, plastic ponies and empty biscuit tins, jigsaw puzzles and lots more really cool old stuff.

Today, Uncle Jack was in an extra cheerful mood. Locked in his van was a very old Chinese vase with birds and flowers painted on it.

"A friend of mine is coming today to look at that vase," he told Gus. "He thinks it might be worth a lot of money."

Gus wished he had a lot of money. He *really* wanted to buy that unicorn.

Gus' friend Joy came over from the stall next door. Joy and her mum, Mariam, were from Africa. At their stall, Mariam gave her customers an African hairstyle, with lots of braids and coloured beads.

Gus showed the unicorn to Joy.

"It's unreal," she said. "Someone will buy it for sure!"

Gus was afraid that Joy was right. Someone else would take the unicorn home and be a part of the magic and the exciting times ahead.

Gus' other market friend was Mrs Tomlin, who sold knitted tea cosies. "Ooh, that's lovely!" she said. Then she whispered to Gus. "Wouldn't surprise me if that was a magic unicorn!"

So Mrs Tomlin could feel it, too!

While Gus was wondering about that, a teenage couple came up to the stall. The girl wanted her boyfriend to buy her something.

"Aww!" she cried. "What a cutie!" She was pointing at the unicorn.

Gus knew the unicorn could never be happy with someone who called him a cutie. But the boy was already opening his wallet.

What to do? What to do?

Suddenly, something was twinkling right into Gus' eyes. It was a glittery letter 'J' on a silver chain.

Gus picked up the chain. "Does your name start with a 'J'?" he asked the girl.

"Awesome!" she cried. "How did you know my name is Juniper?"

Gus didn't know. Was it just a lucky guess? Or had something told him? Anyway, the unicorn was forgotten by the girl. The boy bought her the necklace and everyone was happy.

But then, "How much is this?" A lady was waving a Mickey Mouse clock at Uncle Jack.

"Usually eight dollars, Madam." Uncle Jack gave her a big smile. "But for you today, just four dollars."

A small red hand crept onto the stall. Gus watched as the hand slid towards the unicorn. *No!*

"No, Jeremy, mustn't touch!" The lady spoke to the hand and Gus saw that it belonged to a little boy with red gloves and a red nose to match.

Gus was relieved when Jeremy's mother bought the clock and took the little boy away. He moved the unicorn behind a milk jug, where it wasn't so easily seen.

At ten o'clock, Uncle Jack said, "How about morning tea?"

Morning tea was a Saturday treat. At the market there was a bus that had been turned into a café. Uncle Jack would take a tray and buy a coffee each for Mariam, Mrs Tomlin and himself. For Gus and Joy, he bought a fresh, warm, sugary doughnut.

While Uncle Jack was away, Gus and Joy minded the stall. Soon, they had their first customer. She was an elderly, grey-haired lady and she peered carefully at everything on the stall. Gus held his breath and hoped that she wouldn't spot the unicorn. But she did.

"I collect china animals," she laughed. "Fancy finding a unicorn!"

Gus felt sure she would take great care of the unicorn, but... but....

"Come and get your hair braided here!" Joy had run to her mother's stall and was calling out to the crowd. "Be right in fashion with beautiful braids!"

People were laughing and Mariam was laughing, too. Gus knew what Joy was trying to do, but it would never work. The elderly lady wanted the unicorn. No way would she want beaded braids instead.

But the magic tingle was there again.

"Decisions! Decisions!" Gus' customer cried. "Shall I have the unicorn, or the braids?"

Gus crossed his fingers. Mrs Tomlin smiled at the lady.

"You'd look lovely with braids," she said.

The lady put down the unicorn. "Sorry, dear," she said to Gus. "Perhaps another time." And she trotted over to Mariam to get her trendy new hair-do.

Mrs Tomlin winked at Gus. She knew magic when she saw it.

Gus moved the unicorn behind a pot of plastic daisies. Only just in time, before a man arrived with his little girl. But the girl had already seen what she wanted.

"Rabbit!" she said, and grabbed a grey felt rabbit with pink eyes.

"How much is it?" asked her father.

Gus had no idea. He didn't remember seeing the rabbit before.

"Five dollars," he said quickly.

"All right, Winsome," said the man. "If that's what you really want."

He gave Gus the five dollars.

Just then, who should arrive back but Jeremy and his mother?

"We left Jeremy's rabbit behind," she said.

Uh, oh! Gus had a feeling he was going to need even more magic. Jeremy had already spotted his rabbit. "Mine!" he cried and tried to grab it from Winsome.

"Mine!" yelled Winsome and hung on to the rabbit.

"It is his," said Jeremy's mother. "He's had it since he was born."

"I beg your pardon, but it's hers," said Winsome's father. "I just bought it for her."

"Mine!"

"Mine!"

"His!"

"Hers!"

While the shouting was going on, Uncle Jack came back. "What's all this?" he asked, putting the tea-tray down on his stall.

Everyone explained at the top of their voices.

"That rabbit's not from my stall," he said. "It must belong to the little bloke."

Winsome's father wasn't happy to hear that. But he pried the rabbit out of Winsome's fingers.

"Well, thank *you!*" said Jeremy's mother and quickly took him and the rabbit away.

Winsome's face turned red and she began to howl like a police siren. Tears poured down her cheeks and she blew bubbles out of her nose.

"This isn't good for business," said Uncle Jack. "Sir, your little … er... precious, can have anything she wants from my stall. Nice feather duster? Candlestick? How about this unicorn?"

Not the unicorn!

Winsome stopped howling and looked at the unicorn. Then she reached out her hand.

Help!

Winsome's nose twitched. She gave a huge sniff and her eyes gleamed. From a paper bag on the tea-tray drifted a delicious, warm, sweet, smell.

"Doughnut!" cried Gus. He pushed the bag into Winsome's hand. "There you go! Best thing on the stall!"

In seconds, Winsome had a mouth full of doughnut and she and her father went happily on their way.

"Well, that fixed that," said Uncle Jack.

"Just like magic," said Mrs Tomlin, and she winked at Gus.

Uncle Jack sent Gus off to get himself another doughnut. When he got back, Uncle Jack's friend had arrived.

"Mr Clumber has an antique shop," said Uncle Jack. "He knows all about old things"

Mr Clumber shook Gus by the hand. "Do you like likes old things, too?" he asked.

Gus did like old things, especially that unicorn. But he didn't tell Mr Clumber, in case he decided he wanted the unicorn for his shop.

Mr Clumber peered at Uncle Jack's vase through a magnifying glass. At last, he said. "Yes, that is an antique vase. I will give you five hundred dollars for it."

Five hundred dollars! No wonder Uncle Jack looked happy.

Mr Clumber put the vase down beside the unicorn. Then he began to write out a cheque.

For no reason at all, the vase began to rock crazily. Mr Clumber gave a yell. Uncle Jack seemed frozen with horror. The most powerful tingle zapped through Gus. As the vase toppled from the stall, he made a dive. He skidded onto his knees and stretched out his arms.

The vase fell – *PLOP!* – right into his hands.

"Great catch!" cried Joy and gave him a thumbs-up.

Mr Clumber took the unicorn and gently laid it in a padded box. Mariam brought a chair for Gus, and Mrs Tomlin stuck band-aids on his sore knees.

Mr Clumber patted him on the head. "We could do with you on the Australian cricket team," he beamed.

Gus wasn't so sure. He probably couldn't ever make a catch like that again. But then, he thought, *why not?* There was no telling what he and the unicorn together could do.

Then he remembered that the unicorn wasn't his.

"Thanks, pal," said Uncle Jack. "You saved me a fortune. Tell you what! You pick anything you want off my stall!"

Wow! Oh yes! Gus knew exactly what he was going to choose.

When it was time to pack up their stalls, Mrs Tomlin said, "Well, it's been a good Saturday, hasn't it?"

Jack held his unicorn, safely wrapped up in his scarf.

Yes, it had been a *great* Saturday – a magical unicorn Saturday! And who knew how many more magical days to come?

About the Author

English by birth, **Carol Ann** arrived in Australia in the late 1960s and worked for various Sydney publishers as an editor and author. She now lives with her jazz musician husband in Cygnet, Tasmania, and freelances as a children's author, published mainly by Omnibus/Scholastic, but contracted to write a young readers' series for Hardie Grant Egmont.

CINDY LEE THE INCREDIBLE

By Dan Fields

Miracles are slippery things, difficult to handle and almost impossible to make. All the practice in the world can only help so much. Most of the time they just have to happen. Or not.

Cindy Lee knew the deep end of the pool was off limits, but she no longer worried about what Mrs. Lipscomb said. Not even a little bit. The water felt wonderful, stroking her legs like cool fingers as she paddled from four feet deep to five, five to seven, seven to nine and finally to the white tile at the deep end with the big number 12 in black. She had never been so aware of how the water surrounded her small body. No matter how she stretched, she felt sure her feet would never touch the bottom there. It was a sea at her command. It must be the same, she thought, floating in outer space. It was a place to do great wonders. She had taught herself dozens of small magic charms for getting through the day, but water was her specialty.

All spring, Cindy Lee had worked on the rain. Christmas had been wet and the world stayed that way almost til school let out for summer. She was used to thunder and hardly ever scared of it anymore. Sometimes she had to give her command ten or eleven or twenty-six times for the storm to pay attention and stop. Her chant was always the same: "Stop rain, no more rain." Once she had said it one hundred and seventy three times before giving up. That day, the rain made Mama almost two hours late getting home. All that evening, Cindy Lee had felt sick with disappointment in herself. On the other hand, seven times since she had begun the ritual, the words had worked on the very first try. Once she had shouted it into a downpour so thick it hid the lawn from view out the front window. By "no more rain" the sun shone. On that blessed evening, she and Mama had baked cookies together. Her brother Charlie helped too. She kept the memory stored in the most important part of her. It was the sort of magic that could be counted on in real trouble.

Remembering Mama's baking songs like sweetness on her tongue, Cindy Lee kicked her legs ferociously, trying to start a whirlpool but only turning herself in one slow circle. Maybe if she tried deeper down. Peering across the pool, she saw Mrs. Lipscomb still dozing in the sun. The old woman would have a sunburn on her nose when she woke. That was okay with Cindy Lee. Flipping like a dolphin, the little girl made dive after dive, straining to push herself deeper toward the bottom of the pool with every try. Holding her breath was no problem. What she needed was longer arms and legs.

Cindy Lee clung fast to the belief that one day, when she grew big enough, she'd be able to make the world just the way it ought to be. She was doing pretty well already, even if her miracles had to be small for the moment. There were signs of things changing.

"Look at my big girl," Mama said last week while brushing Cindy Lee's hair in the mirror before bed, taming the thin straight sunshine-colored strands with just a tinge of autumn red. The hair was really getting long now, and Cindy Lee liked watching it fall across her shoulders. She and Mama had the same hair exactly, which was how Cindy Lee had always known for certain that Mama was hers.

Charlie had short dark brown hair, almost black, so he could have come from anywhere. Cindy Lee had told him so once, to sting him for some mean thing he had done, but Mama had told her firmly that "Charlie is ours too," and not to say things that hurt people who are ours. Cindy Lee had not expected her own words to have such power. She'd thought Charlie would laugh at her and had not known Mama was listening at all. Instead Charlie had looked stunned, swallowing hard like something bad had gotten in his mouth. Mama heard everything; Cindy Lee hadn't known before but she sure did now. Mama heard the tiny clink of a cookie jar clear across the house, and she could make herself heard without having to yell. Mama almost never yelled. Maybe at work she had to, but at home she liked peace and quiet best.

Cindy Lee was sure Mama could hear the quiet things Mrs. Lipscomb mumbled sometimes, when she thought Mama was out of earshot. Mrs. Lipscomb was about two hundred years old with hair that was sort of purple and didn't cover her head very well. She came during the day to look after Cindy Lee and Charlie, while Mama went to work. She mumbled a lot, and shook her head slowly when Mama left the room. Cindy Lee didn't think it was nice not to speak right out loud to people, but Mama never complained about it. She told Cindy Lee and Charlie both to mind what Mrs. Lipscomb said.

At night, when they had each other to themselves, Mama was not interested in talking about Mrs. Lipscomb, which was okay with Cindy Lee. Instead she liked to say sweet silly things like, "Look at my big girl." That made Cindy Lee giggle. The doctor said she was just under four feet tall, which was almost big (maybe) but still too little to climb the fence at the spot where Charlie could now pull himself over.

"I'm not so big yet," Cindy Lee told Mama, leaving out the part about the fence because Mama didn't like them doing that.

"Well," said Mama, drawing Cindy Lee into her lap, "let's agree that you're just the perfect size."

Cindy Lee had felt the same way once, but not so much lately. Charlie was getting taller, which put him closer to things she could not reach or was not allowed to touch. This seemed to break an unspoken but important set of rules, for him to leave Cindy Lee behind like that.

Charlie wasn't all bad. He liked to dig up snakes and worms and bugs (the first two were no bother to her, but things with too many legs scared her to death). He made gross noises and peed in the shower. He liked to prove how much better he was at climbing, which wasn't fair because he was bigger. But he was good at reading stories and would usually do it if she asked him, even just as a favor to Mama. Some nights, after long days, Mama liked to go to bed early.

The best thing Charlie did was teach her to swim, sort of. That had been an important part of her summer. Mainly teased her and shoved her in the water for the fun of it, but the determination to show him she wasn't afraid was all she really needed to dive in on her own and not be afraid.

Cindy Lee was pleased with the magic she had learned to work on rainstorms, but she worried that too many spells at once could break things. The summer had gone completely dry, without even a drop of dew in the morning. It made sense to swim as much as possible, because even with the fans going in the afternoon, the house was not much nicer than outside.

She would have really liked swimming, not just put up with it, if not for two things. The first was that the shallow end of the pool was as warm as a fresh bath in the middle of July. Jumping from the burning hot concrete into a piping bowl of chlorine soup sometimes made her sick to her stomach. She only went in because the only thing more miserable would be not to get in the water. An hour after lunchtime there was zero shade, and even though the pool had a swing set, slide and sandbox nearby, there was no way to play on any of these without frying your fanny.

The hour after lunchtime was when they had to go swimming, because that's when Mrs. Lipscomb liked to smoke her cigarettes. Mama didn't let guests, even Mrs. Lipscomb, smoke in the house or near it. Mrs. Lipscomb once told Charlie the cigarettes were medicine for her "heart condition," whatever that meant. If she had told that to Mama, Cindy Lee felt sure Mama would allow her to smoke in the house, but it never came up and that was okay with Cindy Lee.

Cigarettes were even worse than regular medicine because they spread out everywhere and made Mrs. Lipscomb smell even older.

She would sit and smoke and read a magazine and not pay much attention to either of them unless Charlie splashed her feet, or Cindy Lee strayed away from the shallow end, where the big number 4 painted on the tile told her that the pool would be deeper than she was tall.

Sometimes even when Mrs. Lipscomb looked asleep, she would point her cigarette at Cindy Lee and croak in her toad voice, "Cindy! Not so far. You'll drown and I'm too old and fat to jump in and save you." Cindy Lee knew that was true, but she also knew Charlie would help if she did start drowning. At least she only had to follow the shallow-end rule for about an hour a day.

The second disappointment about swimming was Charlie's new friend, a nasty kid named Max Briggs with curly blond hair like a little angel on a calendar, who always had a brand new squirt gun or snorkel or toy car to show off, and used his toys to torment Cindy Lee in creative ways. On the rare occasions he let Cindy Lee play with them, he was bossy. He had no brothers or sisters and borrowed Charlie all for himself when they met at the pool. Max also hated and feared Mrs. Lipscomb, who had no problem giving him sharp warnings if he got rowdy. She called him a rotten little lord when she, Charlie and Cindy Lee walked home from the pool.

Mrs. Lipscomb was really no fun at all, but she spent her days taking care of them and helping Mama, and Cindy Lee loved her for that. Cindy Lee and Charlie didn't like to smoke or read magazines or drink tea in front of the soaps, which meant spending time with them must have been boring for Mrs. Lipscomb too. She always fixed them something to eat and left them alone if they were quiet around the house. Once in a while, she would tell them a story about how much something cost when she was a little girl. Cindy Lee would rather have had Mary Poppins, but she thought Mrs. Lipscomb must be doing her best. Because of her help, Mama could work and make money and come home and fix something nicer for supper than they had for lunch.

Charlie avoided Mrs. Lipscomb whenever he could, and said mean things about her when only Cindy Lee was around to hear. He called her a wrinkly old bat and a flabby pig and one time the 'B' word. Cindy Lee had almost wet her pants, that made her so upset. She begged Charlie not to say it again. Mrs. Lipscomb smelled bad and was not very nice but even so!

"I hate her," Charlie insisted. "She feels sorry for Mama and thinks she's better because all she has to do all day is sit around on her fat butt."

He ran off to climb a tree. Cindy Lee stayed behind to cry a little bit for Mama and Mrs. Lipscomb. Charlie was ten and hated a lot of things. When he wanted to, he could be kind of a butt himself.

Mrs. Lipscomb found her just as she was done being upset, and her breath whistled out in a long, stale breeze. "Oh, dearie," she rasped, "What's the matter now."

That was how she said it, not asking but saying, like she didn't really want an answer. It made Cindy Lee feel very small when people talked that way. She felt her face get red hot and she thought about tattling on Charlie, which would make Mrs. Lipscomb mad and get Charlie in big trouble. Holding the explosion in, she shook her head hard, expecting Mrs. Lipscomb to insist she tell what the trouble was. Instead, Cindy Lee felt crinkly fingers tap the top of her head twice, as if she were stubbing out one of her long thin cigarettes. Cindy Lee didn't look up. Mrs. Lipscomb said again, "Oh, dearie," and shuffled back into the living room. Cindy Lee heard the cushions on the sofa shift around. The volume on the TV rose. The show had a lady with a voice like Mrs. Lipscomb's, yelling about a doctor and some money.

Cindy Lee went to her room and lay down with Mr. Puffs, the big soft dragon Mama had given her two Christmases ago. She did not feel like seeing what Charlie was up to. The TV show sounded like a drag, and she couldn't take another "Oh, dearie" just then.

Oh, dearie.

Lying still with Mr. Puffs under one arm, Cindy Lee thought about how many times Mrs. Lipscomb said those words. That summer it had been a lot. She seemed to be running out of other things to say. It made her sound tired – tired of Cindy Lee, tired of sitting by the pool, tired of their nice house with its familiar smells. She kept coming back day after day, but "Oh, dearie" was taking over her personality.

No longer "Why look at your lovely little farm! Can you color it in for me now?" Not "Goodness, honey. Did you hurt yourself?" And certainly not "There, there. No need for tears." This was how Cindy Lee remembered Mrs. Lipscomb from long ago. Now it was "Oh, dearie, hadn't you better go and have your nap? Oh, dearie, try and be more careful. Oh, dearie, what's the matter with you now?" There was no longer any use in going to her for help.

Diving, kicking, gasping, diving, reaching, each time she went down Cindy Lee felt herself get closer to the bottom of the pool. The cold water still felt good, but she sensed how far away the sun was getting. The deeper water pressed in on her lungs, making it harder to hold in breath. She spent shorter and shorter times under before she had to race back to the surface. She was not afraid, but she knew the pool was testing her. She would have to fight it, the way she fought rainstorms with what Mama called "will power" and what Mrs. Lipscomb called "plain bull-headedness."

Even Mama got an "oh, dearie" now and then. Once, when Cindy Lee was playing with her memory cards on the hall floor, not meaning to listen but just there by accident, she had heard Mama in the kitchen telling Mrs. Lipscomb about a letter or an envelope coming late that month. When Cindy Lee peered around the corner, Mama looked sad about it, embarrassed even. Mrs. Lipscomb glanced at Cindy Lee but did not say hello or seem to notice her. She looked at Mama and did one of her long breaths. All she said was "Oh, dearie," which did not make Mama feel better.

The letter must have been important, because anytime Mama had an envelope for Mrs. Lipscomb, she made sure to hand it over as soon as she came through the door. Mrs. Lipscomb did not get mad when Mama showed up without the letter that day. She just...

Oh, dearie.

It must have been bothering her, because the next day after Mama left for work, Cindy Lee came into the kitchen to ask please for some orange juice, and found Mrs. Lipscomb with a letter in her hand. She had taken it from the pile where Mama kept the mail for the house. It was not open but Mrs. Lipscomb held it up against the window. The sunlight showed some of the writing inside.

When she noticed Cindy Lee, Mrs. Lipscomb dropped the letter right away and seemed to forget all about it. She fixed them each a glass of orange juice, with a little plate of shortbread cookies to share. She acted extra nice to Cindy Lee that day, although she had been frowning at what she could see in the letter. Mrs. Lipscomb's envelopes were always blank and Mama brought them from work, while the letters the mailman brought had Mama's name written on them. Cindy Lee knew the difference. She was learning to read.

Later, Cindy Lee and Charlie had an argument. Charlie had sassed off after Mrs. Lipscomb caught him sneaking snacks. Instead of going up to his room like he was told, he ran and climbed up on the fence, sitting there like a buzzard while Cindy Lee pleaded with him to come down.

"I hope she drops dead," Charlie called down. "She hates us and wouldn't care if we did."

"Don't say that!" cried Cindy Lee. "If she didn't care, why would she come see us every day?"

"Don't be stupid. She does that because Mom pays her to."

A cold prickly thing crawled down Cindy Lee's throat. For a moment she lost her voice completely, then in a shaky whisper she answered, "That's a lie. And I'm... not stupid."

Cindy Lee did not want to believe it, but her mind fitted everything together. Charlie said Mama brought home checks from the bank to give to Mrs. Lipscomb, even though all Mrs. Lipscomb needed money for was cigarettes and hair dye and magazines full of ugly people.

Cindy Lee had worried she would throw up, so she left Charlie on his angry perch and ran inside to the bathroom. She stayed there until she was sure her lunch would stay down, then went to bed with Mr. Puffs and her big world atlas until Mama came home. Mama had taken her temperature, but by then everything was okay.

After a day or two, Cindy Lee forgot some of that dreadful afternoon, because she had begun thinking up new miracles to practice. She could not forget the sickness in her stomach. She did not know the word "betrayal" yet, but in her heart she understood the idea. She had stuck up for Mrs. Lipscomb and now her kind thoughts about the old woman made her feel foolish.

She could not help thinking of bad things she might make happen to Mrs. Lipscomb, and maybe even to Charlie. Not really bad like lightning strikes or car accidents, but things like scraped knees or electric shocks from the carpet. When she was done feeling sorry for herself, she realized this would be the wrong way to use her gift. She thought about trying to make the rain come back, for weeks and weeks like a Bible flood so maybe Mrs. Lipscomb would be carried away over the sea. But going back on all the work she had done to make it stop raining seemed as bad as hurting people she cared about. It would be a waste. Good magic was about moving forward and learning new things. She asked Mr. Puffs about it and he kept his usual wise silence, but he seemed to agree. Let the weather do what it wanted.

Which it did. The next morning, when Cindy Lee was wishing up a few comforting clouds to hide the sunrise, the whole sky had gone black and a hard summer shower came down. Cindy Lee worried that Mama would be late for work, but was relieved that her magic had not broken the rain for good. During the night, she'd had an idea for her next miracle, then forgotten most of it in a dream. It had been about the swimming pool.

Soon after the big rain, the pool was where Charlie and Cindy Lee ended up. They knew that it would be cloudy and pleasant for a few more hours, and Mrs. Lipscomb's heart was dying for a smoke. To distract herself, she'd made her coffee with a raw egg and a lot of brandy in it. Cindy Lee was glad to see her trying new cures for her heart trouble, though the smell of brandy on the old woman's breath was not so nice, either. The new medicine relaxed Mrs. Lipscomb so completely that she dozed off in her pool chair with half a cigarette between her lips. It fell onto the ground before it could burn her mouth, but Cindy Lee had watched, in case.

That was when she'd gotten the idea about exploring the deep end. It might be her only chance to see what swimming out of her depth was like. She was amazed how quickly the water around her feet turned cool, the deeper she swam. Once she reached the twelve-foot end, she knew she never wanted to swim in the shallows again. Maybe if she applied her mystical knowledge to growing some gills, Mrs. Lipscomb would leave her alone about it.

Max and Charlie were horsing around on the deep end ladder, ignoring her, taking turns trying to climb it while the other stood at the top trying to shove him off. Mrs. Lipscomb would have put a stop to that, telling them what a great way it was to crack your head open and drown. If one of them did drown, she hoped it would be Max. Charlie knew things like how to catch toads, and the right way to put peanut butter on toast. He learned that from Mama. When Mrs. Lipscomb put peanut butter on toast, it tasted wrong and Cindy Lee could only finish half. She dove again, hoping to be underwater when Mrs. Lipscomb woke up. They were all out of bounds now. There would be trouble.

She felt herself tiring out for good, but found the strength to push a tiny bit deeper. With her heart beating in her feet, she felt the tip of her longest finger scrape against the rough bottom of the pool. She gave an underwater cry of joy. She did not know exactly what it meant, but something miraculous had begun.

Cindy Lee did not grow gills during her first twelve-foot dive, but it was a triumph and a miracle all the same. She worried for a moment that she might run out of air and drown on the way back up, which would be a disappointment after coming so far. "Faster, faster," she told herself, "rise up faster" with her limbs flailing toward sunlight. To her surprise, the distance was not nearly as far on the upward trip as on the downward.

When she broke the surface, her heart raced, her ears rang, her head went bubbly, and all she could think of was making the dive again. Still a little dizzy, she drew a breath and plunged below. This time it took her half as long to go down and up again. It was much easier. After three or four dives, she could still feel her toes brush the bottom when she paddled just below the surface. *I'm growing*, she realized, a little let down by not having gills but amazed at this new surprise. It was some feeling to know that twelve feet was really nothing at all. Underwater, she was a giant.

Mrs. Lipscomb shrieked her name across the pool, then Charlie's. The old lady was awake, and boy, was she mad. Before, Cindy Lee would have cringed at the sound and probably started crying.

It was still an ugly sound, but Cindy Lee did not mind it so much today. Let the woman holler and squawk and think she knew better. Soon it would be Saturday, and Cindy Lee would come swimming with Mama - just the two of them - and show her how to grow twelve feet tall. Mama let her swim where she wanted. How proud and utterly amazed she would be!

Cindy Lee resolved to start climbing fences and trees, even if Mrs. Lipscomb gave her grief and even if it meant falling off once in a while. If the miracle could work underwater, Cindy Lee felt sure that with a little practice, she could be a giant on dry land too.

Paddling back across the pool, where Mrs. Lipscomb wagged her finger and stamped her feet, Cindy Lee wore a sweet smile. She could not wait for tomorrow, and the next day, and the next. Pretty soon, they would both understand which one of them was bigger.

About the Author

Dan Fields graduated from Northwestern University in 2006 with a film degree. He has recently published fiction with *Sanitarium Magazine, Hedge Apple* and *Curating Alexandria*. He lives in Houston, Texas, with his wife and children.

FINALLY, MAGIC

By Sofi Laporte

Nettie was very nervous.

She had her admissions exam at the Academy of Magical Arts in exactly one hour. She was absolutely sure that she would fail. The Academy of Magical Arts was an elite school that only admitted children of talented sorcerers.

Well, Netty was the child of *very* talented sorcerers. In fact, her parents were internationally famous, known from Timbuktu to Yakutsk and everywhere in between. They had published 231 books on the Fine Art of Sorcery, Magic, Witchcraft and Enchantment and given twice as many workshops and seminars on the topic. They even had their own TV series on *MagixTube*, called, "Everyone can do Magic".

Which Nettie thought was a huge joke.

Because it wasn't true.

Not everyone could do magic.

Nettie certainly couldn't.

She was the black sheep of the family. The only one in ten generations of highly powerful wizards, sorcerers, witches and magicians who had absolutely no magic. Not a single drop. She could not even perform a silly old magic trick and pretend it was magic. She didn't even have talent for that.

Nettie was, simply put, as un-magical and ordinary as anyone could be.

And now she was going to have to pass the entrance exam to the country's most elite magical school.

It was going to be a disaster.

***

Oddly enough, her parents did not worry. Nor did they worry about Nettie's lack of magic.

"She will grow into it," her mother liked to say. "She is a late-bloomer. Some just need more time than others."

"The most powerful sorceresses discover their talent late," her father agreed. He patted Nettie's head and dismissed the matter. "It will come to you later when you do that admissions exam. You will see, everything will fall into place."

"Don't worry, Nettie. If you fail, you can always go to the regular old public school where plain and ordinary people go and get a perfectly ordinary kind of job. As a janitor or cleaning lady or strawberry picker or something," her brother Roland said as he bit into his jam bread.

"Shut up Roland," Nettie said. It was mean of him to tease her so.

Netty's father looked at Roland sternly. "Stop teasing your sister. And there is nothing wrong with being a janitor or cleaning lady. These are perfectly respectable jobs."

"Or strawberry picker." Netty secretly liked the thought of being a strawberry picker.

Roland had passed his exam with flying colours four years ago and now he prepared for the Higher School of Magical Arts. Magic was as easy for him as breathing.

It wasn't fair.

***

Nettie had stayed awake all night, chewed her fingernails to the quick and worried.

What if she failed the exam?

What if it never came? That mysterious magical talent.

Would her parents disown her?

Would she be the black mark of shame in her family tree?

At breakfast, Nettie couldn't force as much as a single bite down out of nervousness. Afterwards, her parents dropped her off in front of the Academy of Magical Arts.

Other children were being dropped off by their parents as well. Many were very well dressed and came with lots of books under their arms, and the parents peppered them with questions.

"How do you make gold from a pile of ashes?" one father asked his junior.

"Whip the wand three times and chant *aureus facericus,*" Junior shot back. He was wearing a little suit and looked like a miniature version of his father.

"Who is the author of the *De potio argentum magicae?*"

"Sylvester Krebus, Sorcerer of the fourth order of Merlin, father."

"Excellent, son."

Nettie felt positively ill.

Her parents hadn't told her to study, they hadn't given her any books to read, nor had they asked her questions to prepare her.

"Just be yourself," her father had told her. "You just have to believe in yourself. That is all. You will see, everything will be fine."

For some kind of reason, that advice didn't really reassure her.

Nettie was ushered into a gigantic room with lots of little desks. She was told to sit down on the third desk in the seventh row. There was a sheet of paper on it.

"When I say 'now', you may turn the paper over. When I say 'stop', you have to stop."

Several minutes passed. Then the examiner said, "Now."

Nettie turned the paper.

Her heart sank. There were ten questions on it. None of which she had the faintest idea of how to answer.

What on earth was a *laurus nobilis*? And how could she explain what it did and whether it worked better at full moon or under daylight, boiled, pickled or crumbled, when she had not an inkling of what it was in the first place?

She chewed on her pencil and squinted to the side. The boy next to her, who was the boy whose father had peppered him with all those questions, scribbled furiously, with his tongue peeking out of the corner of his mouth.

She looked to her left, and a girl with red hair sat there, and after a moment's reflection, she, too, started to write.

Nettie stared at the paper miserably. Time was running out and she had absolutely no idea what to write.

Eventually, she wrote, "I don't know the answers to these questions because honestly? I did not study for this exam. But if you want to know what I know about magic, it is three things: 1. It is hard. 2. You either have it, or you don't.   3. If you have it, you are lucky. And if you ask me, I think that it shouldn't be like that. I think that Magic should be for everyone and there are no right or wrong answers about magic. Magic just is. Or Magic isn't. That is all."

Just when she finished writing, the examiner said, "Stop."

Everyone put their pencil down, including Nettie.

She handed in her paper.

She knew she'd failed.

Then she was ushered to the next room: the oral exam.

When her name was called, she was let into another big room in which five people sat behind a long table.

Nettie swallowed. Her hands were wet and her heart raced.

"Henriette Josephine Evalixa Pimm," a sorceress read from a paper. "Daughter of Frederick and Sybilla Pimm." The other four examiners looked up at the same time. Then they turned to each other and whispered something to each other, then turned back to her again with interest. So, this was the daughter of the famous Pimms. Surely, she would do her parents justice.

Nettie felt so miserable she wanted to run out of the room.

"Go to that table over there and choose your magical item," the sorceress said.

Nettie went to the table. On it she saw: a cauldron, a witch's hat, a wand, a leather-bound book and a daisy flower.

"Go on," she encouraged, when Nettie stared at the objects, perplexed.

Nettie shrugged and picked up the daisy. All five examiners immediately proceeded to scribble something down on their papers.

"Continue," said another examiner. "Show us your magical skills."

Nettie had a huge lump in her throat. She held the daisy in her hand. Her brother probably would have turned it into a bunny rabbit. Her mother would have multiplied the daisies so they showered down from the ceiling in a daisy rain. Her father would have made it grow into a gigantic daisy and then make it disappear in a puff of smoke.

She concentrated on the daisy in her hand. *Grow, grow,* she said in her mind.

Nothing.

Pearls of sweat formed on her forehead.

Right. So maybe "grow" wasn't the right kind of thing. *Turn pink. Or blue, or any other color. Please please.* But of course, nothing happened.

The clock ticked away. One of the examiners scratched the back of his neck. Another one suppressed a yawn.

Nettie went over to the sink, poured water in a glass and put the daisy in the glass.

"There," she said.

"Do you care to explain yourself?" asked the third examiner.

"She needed water. Or she would wither and die."

All five examiners looked at her.

"It's the magic of life," Nettie explained. It was bollocks, of course. But what else could she say?

They proceeded to scribble something on paper.

"Very well. Now, Miss Henriette. Please pick up the wand."

Nettie did so.

"Show us what you can do with that."

Nettie swallowed. How could a little wand be so heavy? It felt like lead. She lifted it. She racked her brain for the spell that her brother uttered this morning. Before breakfast. When he tried to make the glass of milk float toward him without spilling so much as a drop. What had he said again?

It had been something with "Flo".

"Flotasse."

Nothing.

"Flo – Flo…Flotilla?"

That made the wand so heavy she had to use the second hand to hold it up. Nettie's heart raced. There had been a reaction! For the first time, ever, in her entire life, there was a reaction. Maybe she wasn't such a hopeless case after all? Maybe there was a bit of magic in her? Even if it was just the tiniest of crumbs.

"Believe in yourself," her father had said.

But what on earth did that mean? How could you believe in something that you knew you did not have?

Maybe she'd gotten it all wrong. Maybe it wasn't the belief in magic that would do it. But just the belief that whoever she was, she was entirely and utterly fine the way she was.

With or without magic.

It simply did not matter.

She was herself. Nettie.

She felt the leaden coat that had weighed her down for days fall off.

She felt a rush of energy surge through her and all of a sudden, she felt light, so light she could fly. A word welled up from deep inside her. Suddenly it popped into her mind.

"Flotare," she said, surprised. Where had that come from? She knew that that was the right word.

But the glass with the daisy flower remained put on the table.

The five examiners, however, bowed over their papers and nodded, and scribbled furiously.

Nettie wondered why, because obviously her spell hadn't worked.

"Very well, Henriette. You may come down, now."

She looked at him, puzzled.

The examiner waved at her. "Set down the wand, then you will come down as well."

This is when she realized that she was floating at least half a meter above the ground and she hadn't even noticed! With a screech she tossed the wand on the table, and her feet dropped to the ground.

"I – just floated!" she told the examiners with a gasp.

"So you did, not an easy thing to do at all," the first woman examiner said and nodded.

"But I would not have expected anything less from the daughter of Frederick and Sybilla Pimm."

"I floated," Nettie repeated in a daze. "I performed magic."

"So you did," the second examiner said, and pointed to the magic wand on the table.

It sprouted pink flowers.

"I have magic," Nettie couldn't get over it.

"You are a highly talented Empath and Naturipath. An interesting combination. Empaths feel the magic through their intuition. Naturipaths have a deep connection with nature. Their talents are not obvious but powerful. Congratulations, because there are very few Empaths in the world and we need them now more than ever. We will of course be very happy to offer you a place in our Academy."

"But the written exam – I couldn't answer any of those questions."

The woman with the sharp glasses picked up the paper and read her answer out loud. "I think you have written a very fine answer, here. 'Magic just is. Or is not.' You are absolutely right. It is not facts we were looking for at all, but the essence of magic. The ability to see beyond what life offers us. Congratulations, Henriette. You have done very well, indeed."

***

Nettie left the Academy, dazed.

Her parents were waiting outside in the car.

"Well?" her father asked.

"I got in," Nettie replied in disbelief.

"Of course you did, darling. I told you it would be all right."

"I did magic! They said I was an Empath and Naturipath."

"Of course you are, darling." Her parents were entirely unsurprised.

"Mom, Dad, why did you never tell me that I had magic? Why did you never tell me I was an Empath and Naturipath?"

"Because we wanted you to discover that on your own. We never doubted in you. We are sorry that you carried so much self-doubt. But you had to believe in yourself. Because the secret to magic is simply that: belief in yourself."

Nettie digested that. Could it really be that easy?

"Everyone can do magic," muttered Nettie.

"Indeed, darling, that's what we keep saying. And now let's go home and eat some samosas!"

And so they did.

About the Author

Sofi Laporte was born in Austria, grew up in Korea, studied Comparative Literature in the U.S.A., and lived in Ecuador with her Ecuadorian husband. She enjoys writing fantasy and paranormal stories for children and Young Adults. When not writing, she likes to scramble about the beautiful Austrian country side exploring medieval castle ruins. She currently lives with her husband, 3 trilingual children, and a cat in Upper Austria.

THE LOLLY BAG

By Amani Gunawardana

Amelia had spent the last ten minutes hiding in the garden shed. She only had one thing on her brain: eating lollies. Lots and lots of lollies. She put her hand into her lolly bag and pulled out a red jelly frog, a speckled chocolate and a stick of pink musk. In one swift movement, she tossed the three items into her mouth. She gobbled them up like a tornado engulfing a clump of trees.

Amelia shoved her hand into the bag once again. She ran her fingers over something fuzzy.

"Ahhh!" she shouted, dropping the bag onto the floor.

Amelia held her breath as a little creature poked its head out of the plastic bag. It looked like a golf ball, only with purple fur, two button eyes, and a mouth which seemed too big for its body.

"Hey! Stop that!" it growled.

Amelia's eyes widened in shock. The little creature could speak.

"I said, stop eating my dinner!"

Amelia raised her eyebrow and picked up the lolly bag from the ground. "This is your dinner?"

"Yes! And you're eating all of it! Now, give it back!"

Amelia shook the plastic bag and looked inside. There were only three jellybeans and a caramel toffee wrapped in a silver foil. The purple creature wouldn't be happy.

"Th-there's only th-three l-lollies left," stammered Amelia.

The purple creature narrowed its eyes. "Well then, throw a jelly bean in the air and wish me some more food."

Amelia pulled a face. "That's not going to work!"

The purple creature rolled its eyes. "Just have a go."

Amelia took an orange jellybean and threw it in the air.

"I wish for a packet of Smarties."

CLUNK!

Amelia felt a tap on the back of her head. She looked at the ground, wondering who or what had fallen out of the sky. Sure enough, a packet of Smarties had fallen onto the ground.

"Ew! I don't want to eat that!" cried the purple creature. "That's gross! You eat it."

Amelia shrugged her shoulders and stuffed the whole packet into her mouth.

"What would you like to eat?" she asked, once all traces of chocolate were in her stomach.

"Something that's far tastier than Smarties," said the purple creature.

Amelia scratched her head. There weren't many things tastier than chocolate Smarties. However, she was determined to help. After a minute of silence, she threw a green jelly bean in the air.

"I wish for a slab of chocolate with marshmallows, caramel, jellybeans and Smarties inside."

CLUNK!

Amelia felt a knock on her forehead. She watched a big block of chocolate fall onto the ground. She picked up the delicious treat and opened the wrapper.

"This is going to be amazing," said Amelia, breaking off eight squares of chocolate for the purple creature.

"Ew! I don't want to eat that!" the creature cried. "That's gross! You eat it!"

Amelia looked at the creature in disbelief.

"You can't be serious?" she said, with a giggle. "This could be the most delicious treat in the world!"

The purple creature shook its head and almost choked as Amelia ate the chocolate, two pieces at a time.

Amelia looked at the last jelly bean. "There's only one jellybean left. Tell me what you would like to eat?"

The purple creature looked around the garden shed and pointed at an almost empty bag.

"I want to eat that!"

Amelia nearly fell over in shock.

"You want to eat chicken feed?" she asked, looking horrified.

"Yes," said the purple creature, without cracking a smile. "That looks tasty."

Amelia shrugged her shoulders and threw the last blue jelly bean into the air.

"I wish for a huge bag of chicken feed."

Amelia ran towards the wheelbarrow and hid underneath it. She closed her eyes and hoped that it wouldn't fall anywhere near her.

SPLAT!

Amelia opened one eye slowly, then the other. She gazed around the room. She saw the huge bag of chicken feed in the middle of the shed. However, the purple creature had disappeared. She searched on top of the wheelbarrow, in amongst the shelving and even inside the empty cans of paint.

"Where are you, little creature? The chicken feed is here."

There was no reply. Only silence.

Huh, thought Amelia, putting her hands on her hips. *Maybe the purple creature didn't want to eat chicken feed, after all.*

Whistling, she grabbed the remaining block of chocolate and the lolly bag with the small caramel toffee and skipped towards the garden shed door. With the door knob in her hand, Amelia glanced back to scan her surroundings one last time before whispering,

"Where did he go?"

After a minute, Amelia ventured outside never to see the purple creature ever again. Although, Amelia didn't realise, it was still inside the garden shed. Do you know where it was?

About the Author

Amani Gunawardana is a children's book enthusiast living in Melbourne, Australia. She enjoys reading stories that are humorous and quirky. She also enjoys writing children's stories in her spare time.

FINDERS KEEPERS

A Charm City Darkness Story

By Kelly A. Harmon

Assumpta skirted the narrow, built-in bookcase at the end of the hallway and bounced down the stairs in search of another packing box. The slender shelving unit her father had built and stained a deep cherry always gave her the willies. There was nothing sinister about it, but for some reason, the bookcase just seemed wrong to her. Maybe there was something to all that *feng shui* business.

Though it won't matter after today, she thought, since she and her parents were moving out. They were leaving the house her father grew up in—the one *she* grew up in—the one her grandfather had helped to build a half a century ago. All because her parents could no longer afford the mortgage payments.

What a grand way to spend your sixteenth birthday.

The doorbell rang.

"I'll get it," she shouted, abandoning her search to see who was visiting.

She turned the old steel key in the inside wooden door of the Baltimore row home and gave it a good pull. It always stuck in the summer heat. Sixteen panes of glass rattled in the frame as it popped free of the jamb and opened.

Assumpta stepped down into the row home's tiny foyer, as big as a phone booth, and pulled the curtain aside on the outside door to see who called.

"Grandma!" Assumpta shouted, unlocking the second door and pushing it open. Her grandmother was short and plump, and the door barely swung past her on the stoop. Grandma's green eyes twinkled and a bright smile lit her face.

"Happy Birthday, *a stór*! How are you doing today?" Her grandmother spoke in the dulcet tones of an Irish woman whose brogue had softened after many years in America.

"Better, now that you're here!" Assumpta leaned down and gave her a tight squeeze. "But what are you doing here? Mom won't like it!"

Grandma's eyes twinkled. "Well, she can barely throw her own mother out, can she? And if things get really bad, we'll both leave. I wouldn't miss your birthday for anything. Especially this one."

"You don't know how much I've missed you," Assumpta said, stepping back and opening the door wide. "We don't get to see each other enough as it is."

"I know, I know," Grandma said quietly. She stooped and picked up her two large, paper shopping bags. "And us living down the road from each other. Well, you're sixteen today and a pretty grown woman, and I'd say you can make your own choices about things now."

"You don't know Mom all that well if you think that."

Grandma's voice got hard. "Oh, I know her better than you think. Come. Let's get this confrontation over. Your Mom's not going to keep me away from any more birthdays—or other visits, for that matter."

Assumpta pasted on a smile. "Mom! Dad! Look who's here!"

Her father nodded and drank his coffee, leaning lazily against the sideboard in the dining room. *At least he hasn't gotten into the booze yet,* Assumpta thought.

"You're not welcome here today," Assumpta's mother said, barring Grandma from moving farther into the house.

"Let it be, Moira," Grandma said. "She's sixteen. She gets to choose."

"Not in my house she doesn't."

Choose? What are they talking about? Assumpta looked from mother to grandmother; both wore determined looks on their faces. *And could they please* not *ruin the one day of the year that's supposed to be fun?*

Her grandmother nodded and picked up her bags. "If you don't want us to do this here, Moira, we'll leave. But either way it's getting done. And it has to be done today."

"What needs to be done today?" Assumpta asked. It sounded ominous. A sweat broke out on her brow, and she felt a little faint. She didn't know what…but something was going on between her mother and grandmother, and although there always seemed to be some tension between them, it had never been this bad.

Her mother seemed to come to a decision. "No witchcraft. Not in my house."

Witchcraft? Her grandmother wasn't a witch!

"It's not witchcraft!" Grandma said. "It never has been, and it never will be. But keep as tight a leash on her as you have been, and she'll go exploring. There's no telling what she'll bring home after that." She sniffed. "Not that witchcraft is bad… It all depends on the intent—"

"Don't even," her mother said. "You'll have her believing that it's true—"

"*It is true*, Moira," Grandma said softly. "You've just never opened your eyes—or your heart—to understanding that there is more than the grace of the Lord out there. There is a power older than He—"

A power older than Christ? Assumpta thought. *How can that be?*

"It's not welcome here."

Of course it's not, thought Assumpta. Not when she had the most Catholic mother in the world. Who else would name their daughter Assumpta, just because she was born on the Feast of the Assumption—the day that Mary is supposed to have been lifted bodily into heaven? That kind of faith didn't leave room for anything else.

Grandma tried again. "They can co-exist."

"Blasphemy."

The thunk of a beer bottle hitting the counter top drew Assumpta's attention.

And there goes the day, Assumpta thought, glancing at the

clock. *Nine a.m. and Dad is already on the sauce. It's going to be a good one.*

Her father pulled the magnetic bottle opener off the fridge and broke the seal on the beer.

"Help me out here, Kieron," her grandmother said to her father.

He shook his head. "You won't win, Ma," he said, staring for a moment at his wife's face. "She's set in her ways."

Her mother stared at her dad in disbelief. Assumpta understood. Things between her parents were getting worse lately. They used to argue in private, but now her father didn't seem to care what he said in front of her.

Her mom's expression turned suddenly weary, and she nodded tightly. "You win. We'll do it here."

"We'll do what here?" Assumpta asked.

Her grandmother raised her eyebrows, looking at Moira. Moira swallowed, but nodded again.

"We'll see if you have *the sight*," Grandma said.

"There's no test for the sight," said Moira.

"Of course not, love." Grandma moved her shopping bags to the side of the table. Pulling out a dark green tablecloth, she snapped it over the small, oval table in the dining room, letting it float down to hang over the edges of the worn pine. "It either reveals itself or it doesn't. But I have a suspicion you've not even mentioned it to our girl. Perhaps you've even squashed some glimpses of it before Assumpta would recognize it."

"I'm right here, you know," Assumpta said. "I'm hearing everything you're saying." She'd gone from happy, to exasperated, to angry all between the opening of a bottle and the unfolding of a tablecloth. And now they were talking like she wasn't even here. Could the day get any worse?

"Right you are." Grandma gave her hand a pat. She took a seat at one end of the oval. "Sit beside me, dear," she said to Assumpta, patting the chair beside her. "Let's start with some easy questions."

Assumpta slid into the chair and nodded. "What kind of questions?"

"The usual sort." Grandma reached into her bag again. "Do you have vivid dreams? Do they sometimes come true?"

Assumpta nodded. "Well, that's normal, isn't it? Like when I dreamed I would ace my chem test and then I did?"

"For certain," her grandmother said, laying a small spiral notepad on the table, but Assumpta heard a smile in her grandmother's voice. What was so funny about what she'd said? Her grandmother continued, "Have you ever thought something might happen just before it did? Or have you ever lost something and later found it in a place you know you didn't leave it?"

Assumpta nodded. "Everybody does that."

Her grandmother was nodding again, and the smile was on her face instead of just in her words. "How about this: have you ever heard strange noises? A warm breeze in a cold house, or vice-versa? Have you ever had the feeling that someone was watching you, but you were all alone?"

As her grandmother listed the possibilities, Assumpta felt herself grow cold. Every one of those things had happened to her. And more. A single event by itself meant nothing. But consider them all together like her Grandmother had asked, and they seemed to signify something much more...surely a person can lose things and find them, and dream, and hear noises...but if you do *all* of those things...*frequently*...then there had to be something more to it.

Assumpta turned to her mother, watching her slowly settle into a chair across the table from her grandmother, and her words came out more harshly than she'd intended. "Grandma is talking about all those little things you couldn't explain away by saying it was my imagination...or the house settling...or by me being forgetful...isn't she? What were you trying to hide?"

As Assumpta spoke, the blood drained out of her mother's face, and her mother seemed to sink even further into herself. Assumpta let out a deep breath and turned back to her grandmother. "I think you might be right about something, Grandma."

Her grandmother smiled at Assumpta. "Let's see how strong it is with you, dearie."

She took the pad of paper and flipped it open to the first page. In felt tip marker, she wrote the alphabet on it in a semi-circle: A at the bottom left, Z at the bottom right—M and N at the center top—and all the other letters in between, arcing gracefully across the page. She placed the pad in front of Assumpta then reached deep into her bag for something else.

The brown paper bags were large and deep, the identity of much of their contents lost in shadow. But Assumpta recognized a blue silk scarf she'd given to her grandmother last Christmas mixed in with a few other things: some short white candles tied with raffia, some dried herbs or flowers sealed in a plastic bag, and some long sticks of incense. Her grandmother's rifling wafted up the scents of mint and rosemary from the bag.

"Here it is," her grandmother said, drawing a blue velvet drawstring bag from the bottom. She set it in front of Assumpta. "Open it."

"My birthday present?" Assumpta asked.

"An *idea* for a birthday present," Grandma said, eyes twinkling. "If it works for you, I'll take you to a shop where you can pick out whichever one tickles your fancy."

Assumpta smiled and worked open the laces of the bag, then dumped the contents onto the table. Attached to a thin silver chain was a dark, round stone, cool to the touch, with a red bead hanging from the bottom.

"A pendulum," Grandma said.

"I won't let her—"

"Not now, Moira," Grandma said gently, showing Assumpta how to hold the chain and suspend it over the lettered paper. "We need to do a bit of tuning," Grandma said. "Ask aloud any question you know the answer to is *yes*."

Assumpta held the pendulum like her grandmother had demonstrated and said, "Is today my sixteenth birthday?"

The stone began to sway at the end of the fine chain, tiny hitches back and forth—barely millimeters—until it formed enough momentum to begin a clockwise circle. As Assumpta held the chain, the circle grew wider and wider.

"Now we know that for you, a clockwise motion means *yes*," Grandma said. "Ask it a *no* question."

Assumpta nodded. She thought for a moment while the pendulum continued its clockwise spin, and then smiled. Wrinkling her nose, she said, "Do I like liver and onions?"

Her father chuckled.

The pendulum jerked on the chain, swung wildly for a few repetitions, then started circling counterclockwise.

Assumpta smiled. She glanced at her mother who clearly didn't look happy. But she didn't care. *I really like this*, she thought.

"That was neat. Now what is the lettered sheet for?"

Grandma grinned back at her and rubbed her hands together. "Now the real fun begins." She grasped Assumpta's hand and held it over the lettered paper so that the pendulum hung directly over the middle of the page. "We know there are spirits in the area who are talking to you through the pendulum," Grandma said. "If none were willing to talk with you—or if they didn't have an answer—you wouldn't have gotten a reply to the *yes* or *no* questions you asked. So, now you have an option, ask them a question you don't know the answer to, or just start a conversation. If the spirits are willing to talk, they'll spell their reply by pushing the pendulum over the letters."

"Start a conversation…?"

Assumpta's grandmother nodded, releasing Assumpta's hand.

It felt awkward to have a conversation with someone you couldn't see, Assumpta thought, but the way of it was so exciting. She had to give it a try.

She took a deep breath. "Hello," she said to the room, her hand beginning to shake over the paper. It struck her that she was opening a door here that she might not be able to close. *Ever.* She looked at her grandmother who smiled and nodded encouragingly.

"I'm Assumpta," she said. "It's a pleasure to meet you. What would you like to talk about?" The pendulum started to move, a gentle swing at first and then back and forth over the letters on the left side of the page

"What letter do you think it is?" Grandma asked in a hushed tone.

"F?"

The pendulum continued to move. "Guess again," Grandma

said.

"H."

The pendulum jumped on its string and changed direction slightly.

"H it is. What next?" Grandmother asked.

"I think it's got to be a vowel…" Assumpta said, watching the pendulum. "It's swinging too high to be an A, too low to be an I." She licked her lips. "E."

The pendulum jumped again and changed trajectory. If she were looking at a clock, it might be going back and forth over twelve noon. "L," Assumpta said, and the pendulum jumped again and changed only slightly.

"H…E…L…M?" Assumpta said the letters aloud. "No, P. Help." She looked at her grandmother. "Help? Who do we need to help?"

Grandma shrugged. "We need to keep reading the letters."

Her mother leaned forward and pushed Assumpta's hand to the table, halting the pendulum's motion. "This stops now. We don't need to do anything of the sort. We don't know what's asking for help."

An empty pie tin suddenly fell off the sideboard and clattered to the floor. There was silence as they all stared in that direction. Her mother crossed herself and stood, her fingers clenched into fists. Her face drained of color.

"I'd say someone really needs our help," Grandma said. "They don't want us to stop. Let's keep going."

"No!" Moira shouted. "It could be a demon. And you've welcomed it into my home with this witchery."

"It's not witchery!"

Assumpta's nose itched. "Does anyone smell that?" Sweet and cloying. Fruity, but she couldn't quite identify it.

"Pears," Moira whispered. "I smell pears."

Assumpta's father was nodding his head. "Dad grew pears."

The scent got stronger.

"Who did that pie tin belong to?" Grandmother asked Moira.

Moira looked away, silent. After a moment, Kieran picked up the tin and laid it back on the sideboard. "This pie tin belonged to my father. He loved pear pie."

Grandmother smiled. "I do believe your father is here with us."

Assumpta looked around the room, suddenly fearful. A ghost? "Grandfather O'Conner?" She'd never met her father's father. He'd died before she was born.

"Has he been here all along?" Assumpta asked, her voice quavering. She felt distinctly shaky. "Or is he just visiting?" It would be kind of weird if he were here all the time. Did he watch what they did in the house?

Her mind strayed to the stack of steamy romance novels she kept under her bed. Did he know she read them?

Assumpta felt her face grow warm and tried to calm herself.

Maybe he was simply visiting. Like for her birthday. She liked that idea better.

Assumpta's father went to the fridge and grabbed another beer. He freed the cap, took several deep swallows, and patted his chest pockets.

"You don't smoke any more, dear," her mother said.

"Well, I really need a cigarette right about now with learning my poor, deceased father is still in the house."

Moira crossed herself again. "That's not possible. If he were haunting this house, we would have known."

"Not if Seamus had no way to communicate," Grandma said. "I'd say he's finally found a voice."

So much for just visiting, Assumpta thought.

"Well, why should he want one?" Moira asked. "He's been dead nearly twenty years. Why isn't he in Heaven?"

Assumpta let them argue. They obviously didn't care that their words might be freaking her out or that this all seemed too unreal. But could it be true? *Could her dead grandfather be talking to her through the pendulum?*

If he could talk to her through it, could others? People died all the time. Lots of people were already dead. There were probably tons of spirits she could talk to.

She would have liked to have met Grandpa O' Conner. He had grown pears in the garden out back. One of his trees was gone, hit by lightning when she was five. It died shortly after that. The other tree was the largest on the block. It had only produced pears once or twice since her grandfather died, but Dad refused to chop it down and put something else there. Now she knew why.

She raised the pendulum off the table and let it still at the end of the chain, then whispered, "Is it really you, Grandfather?"

The pendulum didn't move, but she smelled the pears again. "I'll take that as a yes," she said. "Wish I could have known you." The scent of pears grew stronger. She smiled, liking this ability to commune with the dead.

"How can I help you?"

The pendulum started its to-and-fro swinging.

"D," she said, then, "F," when it continued the same path. It jumped. "I," she guessed from the direction it took. "M?" It didn't waver. "N, then," she said. "Fin...fine...find–" The pendulum jumped again. And she was much more certain now that the little jump meant that she'd guessed right. "Find," she said. "Find what?"

She watched the pendulum and whispered the letters aloud—confiscating her grandmother's felt tip when they became too many to remember—as her mother and grandmother argued. "We don't even know if this spirit is Seamus!" her mother yelled. "It's probably some demon pretending to be him, lulling you into trusting him. It's not him. I won't believe that. I can't believe you've brought this evil into my house!" Moira shouted at her mother.

"It's not evil," Grandmother said.

"The church says it is," Moira said.

"The church doesn't know the old ways, Moira." Grandma frowned. "I knew letting you into those after-school church programs would be a problem—"

"I learned to sew and cook in those programs! And we hiked on the weekends, and collected for the poor!"

"You learned to turn your back on your heritage!"

"Because it's wrong."

"*You're* wrong."

"And that's why you're not welcome here anymore, Mom. I don't want you exposing Assumpta to any evil."

"It's not evil."

"You don't know what it is—" Moira stood, turning her back on her mother and walked to the sideboard. She adjusted the pie tin Kieron had retrieved, centering it back on the sideboard.

"Then let's let *the finder* determine what's going on," Grandma said.

Moira whirled around, eyes blazing.

"The finder?" Assumpta's father looked up from the junk drawer he was rooting through. He pulled a crumpled soft-pack from the rear of the drawer and flicked his wrist a few times to liberate a cigarette. He put it to his lips. "What's a finder?"

"Assumpta is no finder," Moira said. "She has no power."

"I know you'd like to believe that, Moira, dear, but the fact is, she does. She can speak with the dead, and this one—Kieron's father—knows that Assumpta can find things."

"He doesn't know anything," Moira insisted. "How can he? He's never even met her."

"Oh, spirits sense things, Moira. You know this. Have you really forgotten everything I've taught you?"

"That priest knocked it out of her head, Ma," her father said. He struck a match and lit the crooked cigarette, inhaling deeply. "All she knows is the church these days." He shook out the match and tossed it into the sink, muttering, "Doesn't even know her own marriage anymore."

"He'd lost Lochlan O'Neill's pocket watch," Assumpta said loudly, staring at the letters she'd written down, and wondering who Lochlan O' Neill was. "But now he knows where it is."

The arguing ceased.

"Well, I'll be," her father said, setting his beer on the counter. "I haven't thought about that in years." He whistled through his teeth. "Would be worth a pretty penny right now." He turned to his wife. "That kind of proves the ghost is Dad," he said. "Why would some random spirit waltz in and mention Lochlan O'Neill's pocket watch?" He put the cigarette to his lips again and took a deep pull.

Moira slammed the tin back down on the sideboard. "It could be Lochlan O'Neill himself!"

"Who's Lochlan O'Neill?" Assumpta asked.

"A loan shark and a cheat," Moira answered. "A sore loser. He would want that watch back, even in death."

Her father took a drink of beer and chuckled. "Not likely, Moira. We don't even know if he's dead, though he'd be fairly ancient about now. It's true he was a loan shark—"

"And a cheat!"

He nodded. "Yes—and a cheat. But he was just as amused that Dad had won the watch off him as Dad was. Dad said old Lochlan had patted him on the back and bought him a drink. Told him even an old cheat couldn't win against such luck."

"What's so special about the watch?" Assumpta asked.

Her father answered. "It's made of gold, and the front cover has a ring of diamonds around the edge, surrounding a large ruby."

"I remember that watch," Grandma said. "I saw it at your wedding. Seamus pulled it out every chance he got. Quite flashy."

"How can we find it?" Assumpta asked.

"Use the pendulum," Grandma suggested.

"No," Moira insisted. "It's evil."

"It doesn't feel evil, Mom," Assumpta said. "It feels...*right*."

"That's the way evil is," Moira said. "It makes you think everything is all right."

"I believe it's Grandpop. It would be terrible not to try to help him out."

"But–"

"Let her try, Moira," her father said.

Assumpta held her breath, waiting for the answer. Grandma was nodding, as if urging her Mom to say yes. Would she argue some more if her Mom said no?

"Go ahead," Moira said, her voice low and resigned. "But you'll go to confession tomorrow and talk with Father Tony."

"I will." Assumpta smiled. Going to confession tomorrow was no hardship since she went every Saturday before Mass. At least this time she would have something more to say than that she lied, or cursed, or talked back to her mom.

"Go ahead, sweetie," her Grandmother urged. "Let's see what old Seamus has to say."

Assumpta held the pendulum over the alphabet paper and asked aloud. "Where is Lochlan O'Neill's pocket watch, Grandpop?"

The pendulum hung slack for a second, then starting swinging: tiny movements at first, but growing larger and larger as it arced over the first half of the alphabet.

"G," Assumpta guessed. The pendulum continued to swing.

"H." The pendulum gave its particular hop and changed trajectory. Grandma wrote H on the pad of paper, staring at the pendulum. It swung horizontal, moving nearly parallel to the bottom half of the paper.

"A," Assumpta guessed, thinking the next letter had to be a

vowel. Grandma wrote again.

"Ha," said Moira. "It's laughing at us."

The pendulum changed direction again.

"Quiet, Moira" said her father. He'd put out the cigarette, and his beer sat forgotten on the counter. Assumpta smiled. Maybe these newfound abilities could be a good thing. It was cool that her dad was taking her side on this. Their relationship had been growing more and more rocky lately. Maybe, this was a signal that all would be well between them.

The pendulum's course turned almost vertical.

"M," said Assumpta, and when she detected no change, "L." The pendulum hiccupped, but didn't change course.

"It didn't change, Grandma."

Grandma was smiling. "L again, sweetie." She'd already written it on the pad.

"Hall?" her mother was saying. "How can it be in the hall? I vacuum through there regularly. I've never seen the watch fob, let alone the watch—it's not there—I'd have seen it."

"He's not finished," Assumpta said, watching the arc of the pendulum. The path had moved widely to swing over the second half of the alphabet.

"T," Assumpta guessed, but the glass bead stayed true.

"S." The pendulum jumped and swung wide again, changing back to the first half of the alphabet.

"I," Assumpta said. "H," she guessed again, and the pendulum hiccupped. "Sh—"

"Crap," said her father, turning away from the table and reaching for his beer. He took a deep swallow. "It's the bookshelf. We've got to rip it out."

Assumpta asked her grandfather, "Is the watch behind the bookcase?"

The pendulum hiccupped on the string and twirled clockwise.

Her father tilted his head back and finished the beer, then set the bottle on the sideboard with a *thunk*. "I really don't want to rip out that bookshelf."

"Then don't," her mother said. "It's a trick. Something cooked up between my mother and Assumpta. Assumpta has always hated that bookshelf. Your father is *not* speaking to her through some stone dangled on a string."

"How can it be a trick when you almost never let Grandma visit?" Assumpta cried. "We haven't had the time to cook anything up." She took a deep breath, tamping down her anger. She turned to her father. "It is Grandpa; I know it is!" Assumpta felt her face grow hot. "And I don't hate that shelf, you know. It just gives me the willies. Have you considered that it makes me feel that way because I've always known—at least subconsciously—that something was wrong with it?

"Don't talk back to me, young lady—" her mother said, "Or to your father—"

"Calm down, Moira. I'll go get my crowbar."

"You can't tear it out based on this," her mother said, following him though the galley kitchen and to the back door.

"Sure, I can." He paused to unlock the old door with a twist of the steel key. "I built it. I can tear it out. And I'll put it back again when I'm done." He pushed open the storm door and stepped through the doorway and out into the tiny cement yard.

Her mother drifted slowly back to the dining room.

"Are you okay, Mom?"

Her mother didn't answer.

"I'll go clear the shelf," Grandma said.

They heard the storm door slam and the twisting of the key in the back door lock. Her father returned with his crowbar and his large metal toolbox full of carpentry tools. "Let's get this done," he said, leading the way up the stairs.

Grandma had finished stacking all the books a few feet from the shelf and was dusting it off with a soft cloth.

Her father set the heavy box down near the bookshelf, then ran his fingers across the hand-carved daisies on the front of the shelves. "I do some good work when I put my mind to it."

"You always do good work," said Assumpta's mother.

"Hm," was all he said. Then her father leaned back on his heels, putting all his weight, as well as his strength, against the bar. "I not only nailed this thing in, I glued it. I wanted to make certain it wouldn't pull out the nails and fall forward on anyone."

With a loud crack, the glue on the back broke away from the wall. Her father put down the crow bar and grabbed the shelves with both hands. He forced the cabinet left and right, wiggling it as much as he was able. Then, he grabbed a claw hammer and started pulling the nails from the back of the shelf.

When he was done, he pulled the entire unit away from the wall.

A gaping hole ran nearly floor to ceiling around the wall joists. Bits of plaster fell to the floor.

"What a mess," her mother said.

Her father nodded. "Dad died before he could finish this up. He was removing all the plaster from the walls and hanging drywall. I couldn't bear to finish the job he couldn't, so I put up the bookshelf instead. I always did love carpentry."

"But where's the watch?" Assumpta asked.

Her father dug a flashlight out of his toolbox. "Well, I never saw the watch when I was putting up the shelf, so I can only imagine it's fallen behind one of these joists." He stepped closer to the wall and turned on the light. "Dad slipped here when he was ripping out the plaster. Nearly fell down the stairs. I'll bet the watch flew out of his pocket and dropped out of sight before he even realized it was gone."

He crouched, shining the light into the darkness between the walls.

"There it is!" Assumpta pointed to a cluster of wires where a tarnished chain played hide-and-seek with the dark, coated copper.

Her father carefully pulled the watch upward, tugging gently when it caught.

He rubbed the dusty piece on his pants leg and turned it over. Diamonds sparkled in the light.

"What will you do with it?" Assumpta asked.

Her father pushed the release and the cover popped open. "It's a fine watch. I'd love to keep it—"

"Of course you'll keep it," her mother said softly. "It's a family heirloom and belongs with us."

"Even though it came from a liar and a cheat?" Grandma asked with a grin. Assumpta knew that look. This was no innocent question. "Maybe one day Lochlan O'Neill will come back and ask for it."

Her mother gave her grandma a wry look. "Sometimes you have to take the good with the bad, Mom."

"Like Assumpta's talents, then?" Grandma said.

"Not at all!" her mother said, angry again. "Even if they're not evil, they—"

"Then you admit they're not evil —" said Grandma.

"Moira, Ma…can you both just agree to disagree?"

"No," her mother said adamantly. "I will not condone my daughter's descent into evil."

Grandma *tsked* but turned away to the hall closet, pulled out a broom and started sweeping up the plaster.

"Then let's table this discussion for another time," her father said. "I don't want to sully the memory of this find. Or Dad's visit."

Assumpta asked, "So, what are you going to do with the watch?"

Her father closed the lid and rubbed his thumb across the smooth, burnished gold of the back case. "It was Dad's fault we almost lost the mortgage on this house," he said. "He borrowed so much to tear out the walls and upgrade the electrical…and then all the other projects… Your mother and I inherited a pile of debt when he died."

Assumpta rolled her eyes. She was tired of hearing about their money problems. At least this explained why they never seemed to get ahead, no matter how much her father worked: he'd been paying off his father's debts—and probably some of his own—for all these years. "That's why you watch every penny around here," Assumpta said.

Her father nodded. "Things have always been tight." He let out a deep breath, shoulders stooping. "As much as I'd like to keep the old thing, I think we need to sell it and pay off the mortgage. We'd be able to stay here, and I'd say that's a bigger legacy than this timepiece."

"Kieron, you can't—"

"I can, and I will, Moira," he said. "I think perhaps this is Dad's way of putting things right."

The smell of pears grew stronger than Assumpta had smelled it all day, and then abruptly disappeared.

Her mother's eyes grew wide as she looked around the narrow hallway, searching. "I think he's gone."

Grandma nodded. "I'd say so; his work here is done. He's probably off to Heaven now."

"Good," Moira said. "And now you can leave and take your pendulum with you. Assumpta won't be needing it again."

"I'll pack up if you want me to go," Grandma said, "but don't fool yourself. Today was just the beginning for Assumpta."

"But Seamus is gone."

"He won't be the only spirit Assumpta connects with. She's got talent. And the cat's out of the bag now. She knows what she can do."

"I forbid it. The church forbids it."

"But why would you do that, Mom? How can it be such a bad thing if I can help people?" Assumpta gave her mother a pleading look. "Why doesn't the church allow you to think for yourself?"

Her mother's hand snaked out and slapped her on the face.

"Moira!" her grandmother shouted.

"Ow!" Assumpta tried to rub the sting away. She backed away from her mother, giving her a hard stare, but tamping down all the harsh words she wanted to toss at her. She needed to get out of here for a while. She turned to her grandmother. "Will you take me out to lunch now, Grandma?"

"For certain," she said, leaning the broom against the wall. "If we leave immediately, we'll have time for a leisurely afternoon."

"No lunch," Moira said. "Assumpta has things to do around here today."

"It's my sixteenth birthday," Assumpta said, voice hard. "I'll have lunch with Grandma, and then I'll come home and do what you want."

"Another time."

"Another time won't be as special," she said.

"But—"

"Let her go, Moira," her father said. "The only thing needing doing is *unpacking*. And Assumpta can do that when she's ready."

Assumpta's mother gave her father a hard look, and then something seemed to pass between them. Her mother nodded tightly, then went downstairs.

Assumpta went to her room and grabbed her purse, making certain she had a notebook and some pens inside. She planned to ask her grandmother every question she could think of. Grandma would be glad to tell her anything. Maybe after lunch, they'd visit the shop Grandma mentioned. She'd pick out a pendulum for herself. And maybe some other things.

When she came down the stairs, her Grandmother's shopping bags were packed and she was standing by the front door. Her mom and dad were talking heatedly in the kitchen. She didn't want to know what that was about.

"Bye, Mom! Bye, Dad! See you later!" She grinned at her

grandmother, opening the door for her.

"Where are we going to lunch?" Assumpta asked.

"How about Chinese?"

"The White Rice Inn?"

"For certain," her Grandmother said, her Irish brogue a bit more pronounced. "The shop we can visit is a quick walk from there. And after lunch, we'll go shopping for my special gift to you—your very own pendulum."

About the Author

Kelly A. Harmon is an award-winning journalist and author, and a member of the Science Fiction & Fantasy Writers of America and Horror Writers of America. A Baltimore native, she writes the *Charm City Darkness* series. The fourth book in the series, *In the Eye of the Beholder*, is now available. Find her short fiction in many magazines and anthologies, including *Occult Detective Quarterly; Terra! Tara! Terror! and Deep Cuts: Mayhem, Menace and Misery.*

For more information, visit her web site at http://kellyaharmon.com, or, find her on Facebook and Twitter: http://facebook.com/Kelly-A-Harmon1, https://twitter.com/kellyaharmon.

About the Editor

Amber M. Simpson is a nighttime fiction writer with a penchant for horror and fantasy. When she's not editing for Fantasia Divinity Magazine, she divides her creative time (when she's not procrastinating) between writing a mystery/horror novel, working on a medieval fantasy series, and coming up with new ideas for short stories. Above all, she enjoys being a mom to her two greatest creations, Max and Liam, who keep her feet on the ground even while her head is in the clouds.

To learn more, visit: https://ambermsimpson.wordpress.com.

About the Editor

Madeline L. Stout started writing when she was a little girl and completed her first full-length novel at the age of 15. Mostly, she loves creating fantasy worlds filled with beautiful creatures and strong heroines. When her husband insists she takes a break from writing, she enjoys reading and gaming. She is the founder and editor-in-chief of *Fantasia Divinity,* which she started to give back to the writing community and to help spread great stories. She is the author of *The Moon Princess* and the children's fantasy series, *Once Upon a Unicorn*.

SEE OUR OTHER TITLES FOR MORE
GREAT STORIES!

fantasiadivinitymagazine.com